A SETUP FOR REVENGE

ASHLEY WILLIAMS

URBAN AINT DEAD PRESENTS

SOUNDTRACK

Scan the QR Code below to listen to the Soundtracks/Singles of some of your favorite U.A.D titles:

Don't have Spotify or Apple Music?
No Sweat!
Visit your choice streaming platform and search URBAN AINT DEAD.

Currently on lock serving a bid?
JPay, iHeartRadio, WHATEVER!
We got you covered.
Simply log into your facility's kiosk or tablet, go to music and search URBAN AINT DEAD.

SUBMISSION GUIDELINES

Submit the first three chapters of your completed manuscript to urbanaintdead@gmail.com, subject line: Your book's title. The manuscript must be in a .doc file and sent as an attachment. The document should be in Times New Roman, double-spaced and in size 12 font. Also, provide your synopsis and full contact information. If sending multiple submissions, they must each be in a separate email. Have a story but no way to submit it electronically? You can still submit to URBAN AINT DEAD. Send in the first three chapters, written or typed, of your completed manuscript to:

URBAN AINT DEAD
P.O Box 960780
Riverdale GA., 30296

DO NOT send original manuscript. Must be a duplicate.
Provide your synopsis and a cover letter containing your full contact information.

Thanks for considering URBAN AINT DEAD.

ACKNOWLEDGMENTS

I first want to thank God because without Him I would never be in the position I'm in today. I want to thank my family and friends for believing in me. My parents, Carolyn and Lloyd Williams. My sister Jessica Lane, my brothers, K Day and Preston, my daughter, A'Nealyan, and God child Ca'myria. My fiancé Richard Hatfield, my best friend since pre-K, Shelia Johnson, my best friend since 7th grade, April King. My best friend, Tonya Chevalier; there were many nights I stayed on your bunk and you read my books over and over giving me feedback. Thank all of you for believing in me. A special thanks to Cassandra Ward for giving me the push to make it happen. Lastly, R.I.P to my grandmother Sarah Lee Williams. I love you. And for all of you who are doing jail time and have big dreams, when you return home to your family, remember you can do it.

Thanks URBAN AINT DEAD for believing in my craft.

CHAPTER ONE

Babygirl

My name was Cameron, but everyone called me Babygirl. From my mother's womb until I was about eight years old, I'd always lived in small places. Due to my father's lifestyle, I'd been in and out of hotels all throughout the states. My father, Jonathan, was a pimp and a drug dealer. Before she was murdered, my mother, Wanda, was an addict but wanted to beat the addiction to crack so bad. At least she acted like it.

Along with being an addict, my mother was very evil. She let my father beat me and even tried selling me to his clients without a care in the world. I can't count how many times I'd ran away, wondering why my mother would do this to me. A mother was supposed to love and nurture her child, and with me being a young girl, one would think that would be my mother's sole purpose. Unfortunately, it wasn't.

Things only went from bad to worse as the years went by and as I grew older. Life became harder, and eventually, tragedy struck. My mother was unintentionally killed by my father. He had shot at an intruder who made his way inside our small home, and my mother was caught in the crossfire as she moved about our dark house to safety. She was shot in her chest and died instantly.

My father was arrested that night but was subsequently acquitted of murder charges after all twelve jurors found him not guilty. If you ask me, he should have gone to jail. The murder may have been an accident, but had my father not been involved with shady people who later became enemies, then maybe my mother would still be alive today. She may have done some dirty things and hurt me in ways no child should ever have to endure, but I still loved her. I thought about her often and found myself envisioning what life would have been like had she loved me just a little bit more.

Alice, one of my father's prostitutes, had been a part of my life for quite some time now and I just loved her. My father had been cheating on my mother with Alice for a while and I knew all about it. As a daughter, my loyalty should've been with my mother and I could've told her about my father and Alice, but with the way she treated me, I really didn't care. Regardless of her dealings with my father behind my mother's back, Alice had always loved and protected me. She never condoned my father mistreating me.

She was more of a mother to me than my biological mother ever was, and I gave her more respect than I could remember giving to my mother. Alice made me feel seen and heard. She made me feel like I was special to her. When my mother died, it made sense for Alice to take on the role as stepmother. A role that she embraced.

I sat in my window on a late, summer night watching the streets, and all I could seem to focus on was my stepmother. I watched her get in and out of cars with strangers, collect money, and stuff it in her bra. At fifteen, I knew what she was doing was wrong, but I would never condemn her in my mind or out loud. The hopping in and out of cars lasted a few hours and I kept watch like her bodyguard in the distance. Not long after she had walked into the house, I could hear my father yelling at her.

"Where is my money hoe? Why is it short?!" His voice echoed through the walls. Alice matched his tone, screaming and hollering, making the situation worse. When I came out of my room my father was dragging Alice through the hallways. I watched as his open hand

and closed fist connected with her face. He brutally assaulted her and ripped her clothes from her body. "Bitch, I knew you had my money!" He yelled as he continued his assault with a backhand across her cheek.

Alice always found ways to steal money in order to make sure that I not only had food on the table, but clothes on my back. She knew what she was risking by playing with my father's money, but she did it anyway. After making sure she handed over all of the night's take that she'd worked hard for, my father sent her to her room like she was a child. Satisfied, he left the house, and I immediately ran towards Alice's room. I swung the door open and flew into the room to be by her side. It hurt me to see her hurt.

"Are you okay?"

"Babygirl, I'm okay. You know I'll do anything to take care of and protect you," she proclaimed while holding my hand and looking into my eyes. I felt what she had said was true indeed. I'd always wondered why my stepmother protected me and loved me the way she did when I wasn't really her child. I planned to ask her one day when the time was right.

"Can I get you anything?"

"No Babygirl, just go to your room until I can figure everything out," she replied. I didn't know what she meant by that. I wanted so badly to stay with her in fear that my father would come back for round two, instead I did what I was told.

When he did return back to the house, I could tell that he was both high and drunk. He stood at the entryway of my room and told me he needed to talk to me. I stared up at him with disdain written all over my face as he spoke.

"Babygirl, what Alice did was out of line and I'm sorry you had to witness that. She's been stealing from me, and I finally caught her," he explained. I really wasn't trying to hear it. I knew what she did and didn't care because he deserved it. I sat on the bed and listened to him talk about nothing for a while, making up excuses as to why he needed to teach Alice a lesson, until she walked in. Her eyes were black, her lips busted and bloody.

My father looked over his shoulders and scolded her. "Get the fuck out, you fat bitch!" Him saying that to her broke my heart because I knew he was only being mean and hateful. Alice looked at my father with tear filled eyes and walked away from the door feeling embarrassed, I'm sure. I looked at him with disgust and shook my head. "You get you some rest and I'll see you in the morning." With that, he left my room and I laid my head on my pillow with thoughts of me and my stepmother getting away from him.

In the middle of the night, they were right back at it, but this time I didn't hear my father beating on Alice. I guess he figured she'd had enough. I could hear their heated argument through my halfway opened door. My father threw insult after insult at Alice and I didn't know how she had the strength to sit there and take it.

"Why did you marry me if you didn't accept me as I was, big and all?" I could hear her ask my father.

"I'm still trying to figure that out myself. I'm tired of fussing with you though. If you know like I know, you'll drop this and take yo' ass to bed. I'm still not over the fact that you've been stealing from me and I'm a few minutes off your ass." I only hoped that Alice took heed to what he said and left well enough alone. When I heard no response and saw my father walk past my room towards the back of the apartment, I knew she had.

Relieved, I laid back down and closed my eyes. Before I could get back to sleep, Alice rushed into my room. Her eyes darted around before landing on me. "Pack some of your things, we're leaving." I looked at her and smiled and then looked to my ceiling thanking God for answering my prayers.

Knowing we didn't have much time, I hopped out of bed and scrambled to grab as much of my belongings as I could. Once I was done, she motioned for me to follow her. We ran out of the door as quickly and quietly as possible. Throwing all of our stuff in the backseat of the car, we jumped in and sped off. Never looking back, we left both my father and Louisiana.

We found ourselves in Alice's hometown of Texas, where we moved from hotel to hotel, which was something I was used to. Even if I wasn't used to it, I didn't mind adapting. I was willing to do anything to stay away from my father. Being with Alice, I felt free, and I loved the thought of not having to worry about my father's verbal and physical abuse anymore. That feeling of being free ended all too soon.

One night while I was laying on the bed reading a book, I heard a loud noise. It was so loud, I knew it had to be right outside of our room. I got up from the bed and made my way to the window to see what was going on. My eyes widened when they landed on my father. I watched as he beat on a car window until it shattered. My heart rate sped up when I saw him reach inside the car and pull Alice out. He was yelling so loud, I could hear him all the way in the room.

"Bitch, you thought you could run to Texas, and I wouldn't find you?! You're on my turf and I have people all over this state. Where is Babygirl?" He barked. Alice didn't utter a peep of my whereabouts.

This only infuriated him, causing him to rain down heavy blows on her body. People went about their business as if the scene was a normal occurrence. Scared, I ran and hid in the closet. From the closet, I noticed the hotel door was slightly open. I had planted myself in the closet, frozen in fear. There was no way I could close it and risk being seen by my father.

I was slender in build, so it was easy for me to curl up on the closet floor to hide myself from his sight. The floor in the closet was filthy, but the thought of having to face him made me fight through it. My mind was racing and I had that terrible feeling in the pit of my stomach. I never wanted to feel this way again; at least not this soon. Memories of the night my mother was killed flooded my mind.

What if he killed Alice too? I thought to myself. I couldn't lose her. My thoughts were immediately cut short when I heard him bust into our hotel room. I could hear things being tossed around and concluded that he was trashing the place. It didn't sound like he was looking for me, in fact, he never even called out my name. He had to have been looking for whatever money he thought Alice had and drugs.

I had contorted my body in such a way that when he opened the closet door, he didn't notice me amongst the clothing that hung inside. I silently thanked God because if he had looked down, he would've seen me. Finding nothing, he left. When I heard him slam the front door, I let out a sigh of relief and waited for about five minutes before exiting the closet. Pushing the door open slowly, I picked up on how eerily quiet the room was. All of our belongings were thrown about the room and the mattress was turned over.

Rushing to the window in hopes of finding Alice outside, I panicked when I was unable to locate her. Fishing for my cell phone through the mess my father had made, I went to dial her number and paused. Alice had always taught me to think before I set my mind out to do anything. I knew that if she wasn't here then my dad had taken her and calling would be bad for the both of us. Here I was, a young girl, with no place to go, leftovers in the microwave, a few dirty clothes to put on, and no money.

I thought things like this only happened in movies, but reality had set in really quick that it was happening to me, and I had to accept it. I never knew my grandparents and I highly doubted any of my aunts would want me, so I opted to not call any of them. I was strong for the most part and Alice had taught me how to survive as best she could. I decided that I would wait to see how things played out. Taking my time to put the room back together, I listened to the radio for a while and wondered how many nights Alice had paid to stay in the room. I jumped up after the thought and rushed to the lobby. In such a rush, I almost fell walking in and the man sitting at the front desk giggled a little before asking me if I was okay.

"Yes, I'm fine," I replied, embarrassed. "I'm in room 212, and I need to know how many nights I have left to stay here before I have to pay again?"

"You should know that," he retorted. I ignored his smart comment. I wasn't in the position to go back and forth with this man, so I just waited for his answer. Looking down at the computer, he clicked a few buttons and looked back up at me. "It's paid for eleven more days." I sighed and thanked him, then turned to walk away. "If you need more time, I'm sure we can work something out, if you know what I mean." I heard him say from behind me.

I knew exactly what he meant and when I turned around and saw his creepy eyes staring at me with a mouthful of tobacco, I quickly made my exit. Back in my hotel room, I ran myself a bath to wash off the dirt from the closet as well as the old man's dirty stare. After taking an hour-long bath, I began to think of my next move. In the corner of the room, I eyed Alice's make-up bag, clothes, and Ziploc bag full of condoms. I knew I couldn't fit her clothes, but everything else was a go.

I was still a virgin, but I felt like it couldn't be that hard to use what I had to get what I wanted. Alice had sex for money every night and nothing happened to her. She returned home each night, with tired eyes but for the most part, she seemed alright. I mean, she was right back to it the next night like clockwork. I stood in the mirror, admiring my body, and the thought faded into my imagination. "No way," I thought to myself. "There has to be another way."

The next night as my stomach growled, thoughts of working the streets came back to my mind. With no money and no alternative, I got dressed in heels and the only dress that I packed. I put on red lipstick, put my hair in a high ponytail, and applied mascara and eyeliner just as I'd seen Alice do plenty of times. To look at the finished work, I grabbed the mirror that was left behind. I was amazed at how different and grown I looked.

Here it was a Thursday night, and I was about to do something I would probably regret later. I took one last glimpse at my innocent face and headed out the door. I didn't know the first place to begin so I turned and walked towards the lobby. The thought of that man at the front desk gave me the shivers, but I kept walking in that direction. Surprisingly when I stepped inside of the lobby, it was a woman standing behind the desk and not the pervert.

"May I help you?" The lady asked with a friendly smile. Looking down at my attire, I put my head down, ashamed, and walked out of the hotel without responding. Stepping outside, I was startled by a tall guy with tattoos that painted his neck. I admired his long beard and muscular frame. Figuring he could be my potential first customer, I shot him a seductive look as if I knew what I was doing.

"How old are you?" He asked.

"Eighteen," I lied. He asked me to get into his car and although hesitant, I followed as he walked in front of me. In my mind I was thinking, wow this is really about to go down. Sitting in the passenger seat, I avoided eye contact with him and went for what I knew and started to touch myself sexually. I leaned over and touched his face, still in disbelief that I was doing such things. I went to reach for the big bulge in between his legs, but he did something unexpectedly; he grabbed my hand.

"Why are you out here doing these things?"

Annoyed, I leaned back in my seat with an attitude. "Look, I'm just out here trying to make some money."

"Why?" He questioned further.

"Because I have to pay for my hotel room and buy food. Is there anything wrong with that, mista?" I clapped my hands at him. He pulled out a few hundreds and handed them to me. "What's the catch? And how can I repay you?" I asked with my eyes big in amazement.

"Just stay out of these streets, that's the catch. Next time, you won't be so lucky and run into somebody like me. You will get what you're looking for from one of these thugs out here." I slowly got out of the vehicle, embarrassed yet again.

How can I be so stupid? This had always worked for Alice, but I wasn't her. Heading back into the hotel, I made me way to my room. I wanted so bad to grab the phone and call Alice but I didn't want to regret calling. My dad may have been waiting by the phone or had her phone, and I couldn't risk it, at least not yet. Mulling over the night's events, I laid down and before I knew it, I was fast asleep.

CHAPTER TWO

Babygirl

The next morning, I woke up ready to get on my grind. I brushed my teeth, got dressed, and headed down to the lobby to pay for another full week at the hotel with the money the mystery guy from last night gave me. While paying, I asked the lady behind the desk if they were hiring. To my surprise, she replied yes and asked my age. Of course, I lied and said I was eighteen.

"Have you ever worked in housekeeping?" She asked me.

"Well, I clean my house really well. I believe that would be the same thing," I said, looking at her with hopeful eyes. My father was big on keeping his house tidy and being that I was the only one not out on the hoe stroll, my responsibility was to keep the house up. Waiting for a response, the woman just looked at me with a deep smile.

"Can you come back in the morning and speak with me or the other manager? Also be dressed to work?" I smiled and just like that, I had my first real job at the age of fifteen. I left the hotel elated that I'd taken a step forward. Heading towards the corner store, I planned to buy a few items with what was left of the money the tattoo guy gave me. I never got his name so I just called him "the tattoo guy."

As I made my trip to the store, I got stares from the people on the street that made me uncomfortable. It wasn't because they were staring at me in sexual manner, but because I knew my father knew many people. Alice had told me that her and my father met and began their journey in Texas. And if I knew anything about my father, I knew any new place we went, he made sure to make a few friends. Friends that wouldn't mind giving up information for the right price.

In the store, I bought things I could microwave back at the hotel, a few sodas, and water. On my way back to my hotel room, I kept looking over my shoulders looking for my dad's face. It felt like he would appear at any moment. I hated the fact that I was not only scared but paranoid. I had to keep telling myself that I was a survivor, and I was gonna make it through this.

When I got back to the hotel and put away my groceries, I decided that now may be a good time to reach out to Alice. Picking up the phone, I dialed the number and hung up before the phone call connected. I needed to wait and try calling her from a different number. I didn't want the number to the hotel showing up on her caller i.d. Being alone was the pits and although I was willing myself to be strong, I was still a young girl who needed guidance.

Unable to sleep, I got up and whipped myself up a meal. It wasn't the best meal, but it was decent for someone who wasn't skilled. I'd watched Alice whip up meals on the hot plate the hotel had available and stored a few recipes in my head. Although I'd purchased a few microwaveable meals, there was no way I could live off of that. Finishing my food, I stored what was left of it in the mini fridge. Downing a bottle of water, I laid down and forced myself to sleep.

The next morning, the alarm woke me up around seven a.m. from a deep sleep. I stretched and wiped the sleep from my eyes before finally reaching over and turning off the alarm. Getting out of bed, I headed for the bathroom to handle my morning hygiene which included a twenty minute long shower. When I got out of the shower, I realized that I had nothing to wear to my new job. Figuring that I was bound to get dirty anyway, I opted for a t-shirt and a pair of sweats. Brushing my hair up into a ponytail, I left the room, ready for the day.

"Wassup, do you have any spare change?" A random woman asked me in the hallway as I made my way to the lobby. I began to search my pockets, as if I may have had some change, knowing I had spent the rest of what I had at the store yesterday.

"I'm sorry, I don't."

The girl shrugged her shoulders. "It's cool. I'm Lily by the way."

"I'm Babygirl, nice to meet you," I said to her. We stood awkwardly for a few seconds before Lily turned and walked away without saying a word. I felt bad for the girl. I wanted to say more, but I had a job to report to, so I kept it moving towards the lobby.

"Hello, I'm Sarah. You are?" The lady at the front desk asked.

"I'm Cameron. I'm supposed to start the housekeeping position today," I replied.

"Oh yes, we were expecting you, Cameron. You have some paperwork that needs to be filled out, but we can do all of that later. You're going to be training with Tameka this morning, come with me." I followed Sarah in the back to what she said was the housekeeping stockroom where I was introduced to Tameka.

Tameka didn't seem friendly at all. In fact, she didn't even speak. All I got was a quick nod of her head. It was a good thing I wasn't here to make friends. I wanted to make my money and keep it moving. After the introductions, Tameka showed me the ends and outs of the job and even said I was a fast learner. This job was gonna be a cake walk. I knocked on one of my stayover doors, and Lily answered.

"Oh, hey Lily," I said in a friendly tone. "I didn't know you stayed here."

"Yep, I do," she answered, dryly.

"Okay, cool. Well, I work here now, do you need anything?"

"No, I'm okay," she replied before shutting the door abruptly. Not knowing what to make of the interaction, I shrugged my shoulders and went to walk away. The door swung open before I could turn my cart around.

"Hey, umm, Babygirl, will you let the front desk know that I will be checking out today? It turns out I don't have enough money to pay for another night. I'm going to take a shower and I'll be right out." I took in the somber look on her face and instantly felt bad for her. Little did she know, we were in the same boat.

"Okay, I'll let the front desk know Lily. It was nice meeting you, again." She nodded her head and closed the door. This time, she did it slowly. I could tell that whatever her situation was it was just as fucked up as mine.

Once I got off work, I went up to my room and went to close my blinds when I spotted Lily sitting outside, in front of the hotel. She had bags next to her, so I assumed she was waiting on her ride. I went to the door to check on her.

"Lily," I yelled out to her from the window, "why don't you come inside my room and wait on your ride?" She jumped up from the concrete slab with a smile and ran inside.

I giggled at her eagerness. "Be careful so you don't trip over your bags," I said as she entered my room. "How old are you, Lily?"

"I'm seventeen," Lily replied. "How old are you?" She posed the same question.

"I'm fifteen." I told the truth because she was around my age, and I felt comfortable. Although Lily looked older than seventeen, I took her word for it. "Where are you from?"

"I'm from Louisiana," I told her.

"Louisiana. What brings you to Texas?"

"I'll tell you later." I wasn't ready to tell my story of why and how I got here just yet.

"Oh, come on... tell me why you're here and where's your family?" She pushed.

"Well long story short, my dad is an asshole and my mom died when I was only eight years old, that about sums it up," I told Lily. We sat down and I passed her a plate of nachos that she devoured like it was her first and last meal of the day. I didn't stare at her though, wanting to give her space to enjoy her food. "So where is your family?"

"Well just like you, I was raised by a father and a mother who were both assholes and drug addicts. I ran away when I was your age, and just never returned home. No one has ever come to look for me, so I just stayed gone." Noticing her tears, I reached up and wiped her eyes.

"What's your next move?"

"I don't know, Babygirl. I live in hotels when I get enough money from prostituting. I'm pretty much in survival mode."

"Yeah, I tried my hand at that."

"Yeah, well how did it work out for you?" She questioned.

"Let's just say it just didn't work out and I figured that folding towels and cleaning rooms would suit me better," I laughed. I thought to myself, with both of us having it hard, why not just take the journey together. "Hey, what do you think about staying with me? I mean, we could put our money together and keep a roof over our heads."

"Really? I would love to stay with you as long as it won't be a burden on you. I don't want to invade your privacy," she said.

"What privacy? I'm fifteen, I don't have much of anything going on." I smiled.

"I could find a job and help out around here. Oh, thank you so much Babygirl." Lily reached out and wrapped her arms around my neck, giving me a tight hug. I assured her that everything would be okay because now we had each other. We both fell asleep talking about our plans.

"Rise and shine, it's already twelve o' clock in the afternoon. I made us both bologna sandwiches with cheese, YUM," Lily said jokingly. I rolled over with sleep in my eyes and stared at an energetic Lily.

"My body is so sore. Housekeeping looks easy but it's not. I'm so glad I'm off today," I said, struggling to get up. As I ate my food, I thanked her for the sandwich. "I think we're both overdue for a home cooked meal."

"Well, I can scrape up a few dollars and we can go out to eat tonight," she suggested.

"Girl, we can't afford it. Plus, we need every dollar we can get in order to keep up with the hotel bill," I replied, sounding like the more sensible one out of the two of us.

"Let me worry about the expenses and you just be ready tonight at seven o'clock," she said. It was clear she wasn't taking no for an answer, so I just nodded my head and smiled. "Wait, I have something to show you," she let out and reached over on her side of the bed where she slept. She picked up a paper shopping bag and dumped the contents of it out on the bed. There was two cellphones, clothes, and liquor sprawled out on the bed.

"Lily, where did you get all of this stuff from?" I asked.

"While you were sleeping like the queen that you are, I went out and got us these things," she said matter factly as if she had the money to do so. In my mind I knew the items were stolen, and that we were both headed towards some serious consequences. Still, I decided to put that to the back of my mind, live in the moment, and enjoy myself for once.

"I've never been out before so I guess this one time wouldn't hurt," I thought to myself. Going out in Texas was risky because anyone could be in contact with my father, but I threw caution to the wind and did it anyway. Later that night, Lily and I got dressed and took some shots of the Amsterdam she had bought. After taking my first shot, my chest was on fire and I immediately wanted to spit it out.

"Oohh, careful girl," she laughed, throwing back two shots of her own like a pro.

"Omg Lily, it's disgusting," I told her.

"Ahhh, you're a big girl. Come on, lets go."

We headed out the door to the cab that awaited us. Lily let me know that she knew the guy and had met him on a dating site. They flirted the entire ride. We were supposed to go to a restaurant, but she had other plans and we pulled up to a club. As I got a better look at the sign, I noticed that we were in front of not just any ol' club but a strip club.

She motioned for me to get out and instructed me to stand in the long ass line so that we had a spot. When she finally got to the line where I was, she told me that the bar and food was on her like she promised. She had done what she called a "quick trick" to get the money for us both to eat and drink all night. I handed her the fake id she had me hold in the purse that Alice had left behind and we moved up in the line.

"Damn, those girls are flexible," I pointed out to Lily as we entered the club.

"Yassss," she yelled over the music and pulled a few dollars from her bra to throw onto the stage. I giggled at her antics. When she hopped on stage with the strippers, my mouth shot open. The strippers cheered her on as she did a few dance moves, tooting her booty up in the air which could be seen through the mini shorts she had on. The DJ hyped her up through the microphone and we were both enjoying ourselves. She then hollered for me to join her on stage. Shy at first, I declined but after a shot of liquor she offered, I hopped on stage and started dancing in ways I never knew I could.

"Yes, bitch, I can get used to this," I told Lily.

"Huh," she asked, not being able to hear over the loud music.

"I said..." I started to yell out but figured she still wouldn't hear me, so I dropped it and kept dancing. When the song went off, everybody clapped for us and told us we worked the pole like professionals. A man dressed in a dark suit approached us, clapping his hands.

"Are you both employees of my club? If not, you should be. It's all about money and entertainment here at Debo's," the club owner said to us. Lily and I looked at each other and smiled. "What do you think about joining my team? I'm Debo by the way." He held his hand out and we both shook it.

"Nice to meet you," Lily and I said in unison.

"Are you both at least eighteen or older?" Debo asked.

"Well, yes of course," Lily spoke for the both of us. "When can we start?" She asked, licking her lips. I let her handle the conversation seeing as she was way more experienced in the streets than I was. I knew I could learn a lot from Lily.

"Next Thursday, Friday, and Saturday," Debo told us both. "Come check with me and we'll get you ladies set up. The rest of the night is on me. Consider it celebratory for the new job." It hadn't been 72hrs and already I had new employment.

After getting the good news, Lily and I had to keep our composure. We knew we couldn't be out here acting our age. I also knew that I was biting off more than I could chew and stepping into the lion's den. Life was moving way too fast for me and I knew it would only lead me to some trouble.

CHAPTER THREE

Five years later

Babygirl

Lily and I were still in the streets and even heavier in the strip club almost every night. We both were all about our paper, there was no denying that. I was now twenty years old, with a whole different mindset. Alice hadn't come to look for me in the last few years, but I thought about her often and with the bond we'd shared, I just knew she thought about me too. Lily was now twenty-two years old and as far as her family coming to look for her, that was a lost cause. She was doing it way bigger in the streets than I was. Lily was willing to go to lengths I wasn't, which gave her a name in the streets.

All in all, we still had each other. We both managed to get a place of our own, but you better believe we weren't too far from one another. In fact, we were in the same apartment complex. While working at Debo's, we were able to get our one-bedroom apartments. One would think that after five years, we'd have moved on from there by now, but the money was too good.

Debo's kept my pockets full, and I lived comfortably. Even while working, I made it a goal to study for my G.E.D. I wanted to have something under my belt. Getting that degree was important, but I still wasn't ready to give up this fast life yet. I didn't do much partying, but I did enough. Lily, on the other hand, loved to party. I couldn't lie and act like she didn't get on my nerves from time to time.

Lily stood at 5'6 and had a petite frame. Her skin was the color of mocha, and she had sandy brown hair that stopped just below her shoulders. She was a pretty girl, with a small gap in between her teeth that was perfect when she smiled. I was the exact opposite, still pretty nonetheless. While Lily was chocolate, I was a red bone.

I'd come into my own, now standing at 5'4 with an athletic build. My natural long black tresses fell to the middle of my back and was a perfect segway to look at the perfect ass I'd grown in the last few years. Lily and I had grown up to be stunning eye candy for sure. We didn't look like what we'd been through the last five years, and I was grateful for that.

Knock, Knock, Knock!

"Who is it at this time of the night?" I said aloud, getting out of my bed slowly as if someone lay beside me. Making my way to the door, I looked through the peephole to see who it was. "Whatttttt? I'm trying to sleep," I whined, opening the door for Lily, who rushed pass me with a bag tightly tucked under her arm. "What do you want, Lily?"

"Hurry, shut the door," she instructed in a panic-stricken voice.

"What do you mean, hurry and shut the door?" I retorted but still closed the door behind me.

"Girllll, look, you gotta sit down for this," she said, hyped. The way she'd gone from panic to looking excited had me confused.

"No, I think I'll stand. What is going on Lily?"

"I just robbed a big-time drug dealer for twenty racks, " she boasted happily.

"Wait, you did what?" There was no way she said what I thought she said. "Let me get this straight, you robbed someone then decided to come to my place? And you're happy about it?" She nodded her head. My eyes grew wide and I was both in shock and pissed off at her boldness. "Lily, what if he followed you here? I could be in danger!" I scolded her.

"Babygirl, our struggles are finally over. We can finally move to that big house you've been talking about," she let out. What she was saying about our struggles being over would've sounded good five years ago, but we weren't struggling. And she had crossed the line running to my apartment instead of going to hers.

"No Lily, I'm fine right here. I'm not struggling. I may not be rich but I'm comfortable, we both are Lily! Now you may have gotten me into some shit by bringing that here. We've made it five years, please don't make it to where we have to start all over because you wanna be out here playing stick up kid. I'm not going back to living in hotels." She sat down with the bag still in hand. "Lily, are you listening?" I asked, snapping my fingers in her face.

"Yes, I hear you but it's over and done with now, so let's split this cash bitch and go shopping in the morning." Her nonchalant attitude was pissing me off. I shook my head because it was clear that what I was saying was going in one ear and out the other. "We can buy lingerie for work tomorrow too." I watched as she opened the bag and pulled a few bills out and fanned herself dramatically.

Even though I was upset, the thought of extra money in my pocket was appealing. I just didn't want her to make it a habit of not telling me when she's hittin" licks if that's what she was on. "Bitch go grab some blankets and sleep on the couch. We'll go splurging in the morning," I stated. She jumped up and playfully kissed me on the cheek. I prayed that none of this shit came back on us.

The next morning, Lily woke me up with a cup of coffee. "Let's get dressed, it's time to roll out, roll out." She danced in my face playfully. I smiled and encouraged her with a little dance of my own.

"You talking about, let's get dressed, it looks like you're already dressed... overly dressed at that." I laughed and sipped my coffee.

"Oh yes girl, I been up. I went to my apartment to grab some things and came right back to make sure you were up and ready on time." She pranced around my room, clearly excited about shopping.

We were no strangers to the mall, so when we arrived, we knew exactly where to go to get what we wanted. The stares we got as we picked up the latest fashions from Christian Dior to Givenchy didn't phase us a bit. If anything, it made us want to ball harder. Lily was really showing out when she suggested going into the sex store. I laughed as she picked up different dildos and other sex toys and held them up for me to see. She was in her element.

As popular dancers at Debo's, people knew us locally. It seemed that every store we went into, we found ourselves waving at people who frequented the club. We had so much fun shopping and eating that I almost forgot that we were spending money that Lily had stole. When we made it outside to wait for our cab to arrive, I noticed Lily pulling outfits and sex toys from her big tote bag.

"Really Lily, you got money and you're still stealing? That explains why everyone was staring at us!"

"No, they were staring because we're familiar faces. And, yes bitch, I'm still me and just because I have a little money, I ain't gon' forget where I come from. This ain't even enough money for me to forget." I didn't agree with her at all and I was embarrassed.

Deciding to let it go, I waited for the cab in silence. We made it back to our apartment building with all of our bags. And by the time we entered my house, I was over being upset. Lily was going to be Lily just as she'd said and I'd been putting up with it this long so, what the hell.

"Girl, we have got to get us a car so we won't have to waste all of our energy waiting for a cab to come pick us up. We are both too small to be breathing so hard." We both bust out laughing.

"Well, we still have about twelve thousand dollars left, I'm sure we could go get us something decent to get around in," she said.

"Hell yeah, now you are speaking my language." Getting a car was our next level. Oooh, I couldn't wait to pull up to the club in our new shit.

We tried on our new outfits while getting ready to go into the club. I noticed that Lily's phone seemed to be ringing more than usual. Whoever was calling just kept hanging up when she answered. All kinds of thoughts went through my head, the one that rang the loudest was, could it have been the dealer she'd stolen from calling? It didn't seem to bother Lily at all so I tried to adapt that same attitude and not let it phase me.

Lily had taken her turn up to the next level. I watched as she pulled a small baggy from her bra and took a seat at my kitchen table with it. I knew coke when I saw it. In my parents' line of business, there was a lot of nose playing going on. I didn't judge but when she asked me if I wanted to indulge, I quickly shut her down. I was slightly offended but didn't let on that I was. The high had her on one because she began rambling about some man out of nowhere.

"Why is it that the man I really want doesn't want me? It's always, 'I need to gain a little weight and get braces for my teeth.' He's so critical of my appearance. All I have is a little gap, and it's average looking. And what's wrong with my weight? Most men like petite women, what's wrong with me? Why doesn't he want me?" It seemed as though she'd aged a few years as the tears ran down her cheeks. She really needed to lay off the drugs. It was starting to make her emotional. As I went to respond to her meltdown, she kept going. "I would do anything for him. I'll stop stealing, tricking with all these men, and even stop working at the club."

"Stop it!" I yelled. "You shouldn't stop all those things for a man. Those things you should want to stop for yourself."

"You don't understand, Babygirl. When I do those things, I feel love."

"Wait, getting drunk and high make you feel love?" She nodded her head and I felt for her. Pulling her in for a hug, I rubbed her back in an effort to comfort her. Our pregaming had taken a turn and we needed to get back on track because we had work to do. I chose to drop the conversation for now and focus on that.

On our way to the club, I thought about Lily's breakdown. While she was vying for love from a man, I wanted that from my father. Growing up, I thought my dad hated me because he'd made it clear that he wanted a son. I grew to realize he was just a hateful mother-fucker who dealt with me because he had to. He was just as verbally abusive with me as he was with his women.

Sad to say, in a way, he treated me like one of his hoes. He was nice when he wanted to be but rarely if ever showed me any love.

Deep down inside I was hurting so badly. A daughter's first love was her father. Unfortunately for me, my father had aided in my first heartbreak. I quickly snapped out of it when I noticed that we'd arrived at the club. I looked over at my overly drunk friend and shook my head.

"Let's roll," Lily said, seeming to have found a burst of energy. I hopped out of the cab right behind her and we strolled into the club.

"Everybody in the club getting' tipsy."

Lily and I bopped through the crowed as the music played. We both headed straight to the back, opting out of stopping at the bar like we usually did because we had already drank back at the house. Before we made it to the back, I heard a voice call out to us.

"Hey, you in the pink." I glanced at Lily and she gave me a silly look.

"Girl, he's talking to you," I said to her.

"Bitch, he's talking to you in the pink. I know my colors." I giggled at her response and turned to get a good look at the man who'd called out to me. He sat only a couple feet away with a champagne glass in his hand.

"How may I help you?" I asked professionally once I made it over to him.

"You don't notice me? I come to watch you dance every time you hit that stage," the man said, pointing towards the stage.

"I've seen you around here before, but I vaguely remember who you are," I lied.

"I'm Christian, and you are? And I already know your stage name so how about we try your real name?" He held his hand out for me to shake.

"Cameron," I replied, accepting his hand.

"Christian and Cameron, that sounds good together." I blushed at his smooth talk.

"Everyone calls me Babygirl." I smiled.

"Cameron is a beautiful name, but I'll call you Babygirl if that's what you prefer," Christian said, giving my hand a sweet peck.

"I want to take you out to dinner, Cameron."

"Straight to the point, huh?" I blushed, hiding the fact that his forwardness gave him a leg up in my book. So as not to seem thirsty, I didn't want to give him a yes too quick.

"It's who I am. When I see something I want or in this case that I'm interested in, I don't see the point of beating around the bush."

"I like the way you think. Dinner sounds nice, so yes. For now, duty calls. I'll catch up with you after my performance, okay?" Christian nodded his head, and I walked off.

"Aye," he called out to me.

"Yes?" I turned to see what he wanted.

"Do my favorite move when you get up there."

"And which move might that be, Christian?" I smirked, letting his name roll off my tongue.

"The one when you climb all the way to the top, flip upside down, and land in a hard split while looking back at me." He knew the move in detail. If I wasn't sure that he was watching before, I definitely knew now.

"That would be my signature move. I'll be sure to include that in my performance just for you." I smiled and walked off.

I replayed our interaction in my mind as I headed to the back where the locker rooms were. Christian was tall, standing at about 6'1, he had rich, chocolate skin, and tattoos that covered the parts of his body I could see. Two full sleeves and his neck. I took note of his pretty, white teeth and the golds at the bottom. He appeared to be in shape with the physique of a body builder. His body would match perfectly with mine, I imagined.

"Bitch you look happy," Lily said, coming behind me as I got dressed to go on stage. "What that man say to you?"

"His name is Christian," I responded in awe. "And he didn't have to say much." I took a shot of gin and headed for the stage door.

"Coming to the stage is our personal stallion, Babygirl!!"

I could hear the announcer say through the speakers. I hit the stage in red bottom pumps, a black see-through dress, and long black stockings that came up to my thighs. The red lipstick made my lips look even more plumped and kissable. It was typical for strippers to have their hair out to swing as they danced, but I decided to go with a bun tonight. With low, seductive eyes, I eyed my audience.

I scanned the room and my eyes locked in on my target, my newfound number one fan, Christian. I wasted no time surrendering to his request. As I hit my signature move I glared back at Christian with lust filled eyes. Staring at him made my body heat up and it only turned up more when he damn near threw his whole wallet on stage. The stage was covered in green faces and I made sure to scoop them all up. He stopped me as I headed for the back.

"What's your taste in men?" He asked bluntly.

"Well, right now, my taste is you," I replied with a smile. Christian smiled back and gave me a business card with all of his contact info on it.

"Real estate, huh?" I said, reading the card. Judging by the entourage he sat with, I knew that the real estate business was just a front.

"Call me," he said, walking off with his fellas following his lead. I watched him until he disappeared into the crowd.

"Girl, come on so we can call it a night," Lily said from behind me. I followed her and we changed over to our street clothes before heading out. I was glad that Christian had left before us because I didn't want him to see me get into a cab.

"Man fuck you, pay me." Lily and I could hear voices coming from side of the building as we walked out. I wasn't trying to be nosey, but I was able to place Christian's voice immediately. And he was the aggressor, demanding the money.

"Oh, shit Lily, that's Christian. Let me get a little close to see what's going on."

"And get your brains blown out? You must be bat shit crazy!" Lily exclaimed, finally saying something that made sense. Just as I went to say something else, we heard two gunshots and watched as people scattered like roaches. "Girl, come the hell on!" Lily grabbed my arm and I went hesitantly.

I glanced back and spotted Christian and his entourage as they came from behind the building with guns. It was a good thing that Lily and I kept a good pace because had they seen us, there was no telling what could've happened. A block over, we flagged down a cab and hopped in it. Only after I was seated did I realize my heartbeat was racing.

When we made it back to our apartment complex I crashed at Lily's spot. My apartment was an upstairs and I was just too exhausted to climb anything else tonight. I laid down and took Christian's business card out and called him. His phone rang twice and went straight to voicemail. I sighed thinking about what he may have gotten himself into. I was too exhausted to wait up and see if he would call me back.

This guy would be nothing but trouble, I could feel it. Even knowing that, I was still open to the dinner invitation. I wanted to test those troubled waters.

CHAPTER FOUR

Lily

It was a Sunday night and I found myself in my lover's apartment with my legs touching my ears and his face buried in my wetness. My high-pitched moans could be heard throughout the room. It seemed as if my orgasm was never ending.

"Oh Tommy, don't stop! Right there! Eat this pussy, nigga!" Tommy complied with my commands and ate me like I was his last meal. He made sure to get every last drop that I squirted into his mouth. I looked down at him through hooded eyes as my sex thumped and licked my lips.

While Tommy may have acted like he didn't share my feelings when it came to how much I loved him, he never neglected to show me when we were in the bedroom. Our love making was powerful. Every time he touched me, I felt a tingling sensation from my head, down to my toes. He didn't consider it love making and often clowned me when I said it. According to him, we were straight fucking, but I knew better.

"Mmm, yeah, cum for me, bitch," he let out while sliding his finger up and down my slit. I felt my juices slide down the crack of my ass.

"Sssss, papi, I want to try something different. I want you to open this asshole up and fuck me in my ass." He was happy to oblige, without a word spoken. He turned me around and bent me over so that my ass was tooted up in the air. It wouldn't have been the first time I'd tried anal in my life. Shit, I've done just about everything me and Tommy had done. I wouldn't tell him that though. He spat on my ass and proceeded to rub it in a circular motion with his thumb before sliding it in. "Oohhhh yes," I crooned from the pleasure.

"Nice and tight," he complimented before giving my ass a slap. "I'm gonna fill your asshole up, Lily. You betta not run." I didn't respond verbally but nodded my head. Feeling that I'd had enough of his thumb, he replaced it with his dick, sliding in slowly, making me bite down on my lip at the mixture of pleasure and pain.

"Oohh, shiitttt," I let out and pushed my ass back a little to take in more of him. It didn't take long to get in the groove of things and before I knew it, he was fucking me hard up against the headboard. "Ahhh, shit yeah!" We went at it for a few before switching positions, where I got on top and rode him like I was a part of the Kentucky Derby. When I looked down at Tommy's contorted face, I knew that he was pleased with my performance.

If I knew how to do anything, I knew how to fuck like nobody's business. I knew I was doing my thing. I grabbed at my own titties as I felt another orgasm rip through my body. I did kegels, making him skeet his nut into my awaiting pussy.

"Goddamn, that was the best dick I ever had!" I said breathlessly. I climbed down slowly off of him and rolled over.

"Yeah, you got some good shit yourself, mami. I swear if you gained a few and closed that gap up, you'd be a winner. That pussy is a pot of gold." As if he hadn't just insulted me with a backhanded compliment, Tommy stood up and headed to the bathroom.

We'd just had a good time and he just had to fuck it up. Over his constant criticism, I decided that he'd just have to get done like my other vics. I didn't have to put up with his shit. Doing what I did best, I moved quickly, picking up anything he had of value and throwing it inside my purse. I glanced up at the flat screen tv and thought to myself that a bigger bag would've been nice and giggled to myself.

"Are you okay in there?" Tommy asked.

"Yes baby, I'm just waiting on you," I replied in an innocent tone, never stopping my movement.

"I'll be out in just a second," he yelled out.

"Good... that gives me a second more to rob yo' stupid ass," I whispered to myself as I roamed around the room. Clearly, I was moving too fast because I ended up stubbing my toe on his coffee table. "Shit!" I whispered, loudly.

"You stealing from me bitch?!" Tommy barked, making me jump and drop my purse. My eyes stayed locked in with his as I froze. I was caught red handed and speechless. Feeling it was best to make a run for it, I snatched the bag and went to make a move, only to be snatched back by my hair. "Bitch I should kill you!" Tommy spat and showered my face with his saliva. He snatched my Coach bag from my hand and I went to reach for it.

"Wait! I'll give you your shit!" I pleaded. He ignored my pleas and opened the bag to see his jewelry, wallet, and even a pair of his boxers.

"My boxers, really bitch?" I was embarrassed and scared out of my mind. He continued to raid my bag while still having a good grip on my hair. I watched as he pulled out more items, until he got to the white envelope I had, which held the money in it for mine and Babygirl's car.

"No, that's all of the money I have, please don't take it!" I cried out.

"Fuck you, it's mine. You called yourself stealing from me and now, I guess the joke's on you, now get the hell up out my spot!" There was no way I was giving up that envelope without a fight. To his surprise, I maneuvered out of his grasp and bit his arm.

He smirked like he was egging me on. I went to grab the envelope and he pulled me into a bear hug so tight, I could barely breathe. Fuck this, I thought to myself while throwing my head back, hitting him in the face. He loosened his grip and we tussled. Eventually getting the best of me when he grabbed hold of my neck, Tommy pushed me towards the door and out of his room.

"Fuck you, Tommy!" I yelled from the floor, in the hallway of his building.

"Yeah, whatever, you stupid thieving bitch! And my name ain't Tommy!" He slammed the door so hard it made me jump. Hurt and broke, I got my bearings, stood up, and limped towards the elevators. This was some bullshit.

It was one am, and I found myself pacing my apartment floors, racking my brain to see how I was going to get the car money back. What happened to me tonight had never happened before. It just showed me that for as slick as I thought I was, there was someone slicker. Shit, this man's name wasn't even Tommy and here I was thinking I was in love. I was a damn fool, that's what I was, but I had no time to wallow in self pity. I needed to make that 12k back, quick.

My pacing went on until about seven am and even then, I still hadn't come up with a solid plan. Sleep was the last thing on my mind. I'd taken a bump of coke that aided in my ability to be wide awake. I was supposed to wake Cameron up at eight to take a trip with me to the bank, but since I had no money to put in the account, I decided not to say anything. I was gonna figure this shit out.

I got dressed and headed out the door. Walking into the bank, my eyes scanned the place and stopped at the line to get to the teller. Getting on the line, I thought about how I could rob the bank and no one would ever know it was me. I took note of how the bank tellers moved as well as the security guards. While the tellers were jovial in their greetings, I could tell that they were just trying to pass the time. The security guards looked to be middle aged men who I was sure could be easily seduced with a piece of pussy. I kept this all in mind as I made it up to the teller window.

"Hello, how may I help you?" A young black woman dressed in a stiff blazer asked.

"Hello," I returned her greeting, just as pleasant. "I would like to apply for a loan."

"Okay, I can get someone to assist you with that. Do you have an active checking account with us that's been open for at least 90 days?" The teller asked.

"No, I don't have an account with you."

"Oh, I see. I apologize but one of the requirements for opening a loan with us is you must have an account. I'd be happy to have someone sit down with you to open an account and you can come back in 90 days to apply for your loan."

That wasn't what I wanted to hear, so rather than responding, I turned on my heels and left the building. Standing outside of the bank, I called for a cab. The thoughts of robbery swam around in my head. I just knew that with proper planning, I'd be able to take the bank. All I needed was time to put it all together in my head and I could make it happen. The cab driver pulled up and I hopped in the backseat.

I wanted to call Babygirl and tell her what was going on, but she had a way of making situations worse than what they appeared to be. Granted, me getting our car money taken was serious, but I needed her to focus more on the solution instead of the problem. That's the part I played in our duo, I came up with the solutions for the most part. My methods weren't always the best, in the same token, I got results. Hence the reason why we were still going strong at the club.

"Hey, you can let me out right here," I said to the cab driver.

"Okay, no problem." He pulled over and stopped the car. I handed him my cab fare and didn't step out immediately. "Alright ma'am, you be safe and enjoy the rest of your night." The dusty bearded man spoke, clearly wanting to get rid of me.

"Hey, you in the mood for a good time?" I asked, licking my lips. He watched me through the rearview mirror. "It won't cost you much, and I promise to make it worth your while."

"No. Now if you would please exit my car." He kept his eyes on me and I figured I'd turn it up a notch in an effort to persuade him.

I lifted my shirt up, exposing my titties. "Are you sure you want me to get out?" I spoke seductively.

"Get the hell out of my car!" He demanded and I got the hint. Quickly pulling my shirt down, I got out. He sped off before I could fully get on the sidewalk.

Looking up at the hotel I had him drop me in front of, I shook my head. I couldn't go back home knowing that I'd fucked up. At the front desk, I paid for a two night stay to get my mind right without interruption. The cab driver was an ass, but he'd regret turning me down once he noticed that his wallet that he had resting on his center armrest was gone. He'd unknowingly paid for my hotel stay.

I was a true pro at this shit. When I made it to my room, I used my phone to browse one of the online dating sites I frequented.

Usually, I was only active online for a good time. I never had the intention on robbing my dates, but if they weren't willing to give to me voluntarily, then I was willing to take their money and whatever else had value, involuntarily.

"Mmmm, well look at this fine piece of man," I said out loud while browsing a website that I wasn't familiar with. I sent him a message with an open invitation for him to come over and play and he responded immediately. I took a quick shower and wrapped a hotel robe around my body. There was no need to redress, I would only end up naked. Plus I didn't have anything to wear other than what I came with.

A knock at the door let me know that it was showtime. I ran over and opened the door. The guy was dressed in a blue polo shirt, black jeans that fit him tightly, and black cowboy boots didn't look quite the same in person as he did in his profile pic. He wasn't my type either, but I figured he could afford me. Shutting the door, I got ready to get down to business.

"Tonight, it's my world and you're just living in it, you understand?" I made clear. He nodded his head and I smirked, knowing I was about to take him on the ride of his life.

CHAPTER FIVE

Babygirl

I sat up in my bed, calling Lily's phone off the hook, only to receive her voicemail again. With my frustration mounting, I gave up and called a different number.

"Whoa now," Christian answered.

"Hi Christian, it's Babygirl. We met the other night at the club," I said, nervously.

"Of course, how could I forget. What took you so long to call?" He asked.

"Well, I called you the same night when I made it back home but no answer, so I was waiting for you to return my phone call."

"My bad about that, ma. I've been so busy with my businesses... it must've slipped my mind to return your call."

"Yeah, I get it. I've been pretty busy myself. I have been trying to locate my friend, we were supposed to get together yesterday but still no answer from her either. I guess everybody has been ignoring me." I said jokingly.

"Oh naw, ma... it's nothing like that, and I'm sure your friend will show face soon."

"Aye O'block, let's roll." I could hear someone say in the background.

"Who is O'block?" I questioned, nosily.

"Oh that's what the streets call me," Christian told me.

"Oh, how come you didn't tell me that? Am I not special enough to know?" I smiled at my subtle flirting.

"Didn't feel there was a reason to. My street name comes with a lot of shit, so you may wanna just refer to me as Christian. I don't wanna scare you off."

"I'm not scared," I made clear. "I'm a big girl."

He chuckled. "I hear you. Look, I'm sorry to cut our conversation short but I gotta handle something. When can I take you out?"

"When would you like to take me out? You asked me on a date remember, I'll go along with your plans."

"How about tomorrow evening, 8:oo sharp?"

"Sounds good to me."

We both hung up the phone and I hugged my pillow all giddy and shit. That quick I had forgotten about what happened at the club. I was looking forward to my dinner date with Christian. Hearing his voice put me in a good mood. Now all I needed was for Lily to pick up her damn phone and I'd be in an even better mood.

I was beginning to worry and didn't know whether to call the police or what. Not wanting to overreact, I dialed her number again and still no answer. As I went to lock my screen, the picture on my home screen of me and Alice made me pause. I felt myself tearing up. Although five years had passed since I'd seen her, there wasn't a day that went by where she didn't cross my mind.

I often wondered how she was doing and if she was still alive. Knowing my father, there was no telling. Locking my phone, I turned the ringer on loud and put it on my night stand. I wanted to be able to hear it in the middle of the night in case Lily called. This girl was gonna be the death of me. Wherever she was I just hoped she was okay. I laid down and willed myself to sleep thinking about Christian and what would come of our date.

I dreaded the part where he may ask me personal questions about myself. There was no way I was gonna tell him that I had no family outside of Lily or any of my family history for that matter. I kinda hoped that he would keep it light and ask about my favorite food and color. Something where it didn't require me having to go back to that place that once broke me. I couldn't go back there mentally.

Here it was Wednesday night, and I still hadn't heard from Lily. It was rare that we went this long without talking. I'd even gone to her apartment, and she wasn't there. Wherever she was, when she did turn up, I was going to curse her out. I needed to have a clear head for dinner with Christian so again, I put worrying about Lily's grown ass to the back of my mind. My cell phone rang as I put the final touches on my outfit and Christian's name appeared on the screen.

"You're on time huh?" I pointed out once the call connected. "I like that."

He laughed a little. "I got your text earlier, so I had to make sure I was on my shit. Come outside, I'm here." The way he spoke with authority made me want to do whatever he said.

"I'll be right out," I told him before hanging up. I took one last look at my bangin' body and was more than satisfied with what I'd put together. I wore a tight, short, black dress, black heels, gold accessories, and a gold clutch. My hair was bone straight and I looked edible.

Leaving my apartment, I thought to check Lily's apartment again. As I went to do so, I stopped mid step and about faced. At this point, if she hadn't reached out or answered any of my calls, it was clear she didn't want to be found. It still didn't make me worry any less but right now, I wanted to put my wants and needs first. And I wanted and needed Christian at the moment.

I had no idea what kind of car to look for Christian in, so I pulled my phone out to call him. Just as I went to press his contact, a blacked-out Cadillac Escalade pulled up and stopped about five feet away from me. Of course, I stopped what I was doing to see who would be rolling up in the all black beauty. The back door opened, and to my surprise, Christian hopped out if it, exuding the confidence of an important man.

"Oh my God, this is stunning," I let out while taking strides towards him.

"For you, boo. I had to make this night special for a very special lady." He smiled and for the first time, I took notice of the dimples in his cheeks. The man was fine. He helped me into the truck and when I sat down, I let out a satisfied sigh. The seats felt like butter.

We arrived at an upscale restaurant in the big city of Dallas about 45 minutes from my apartment. Christian showed that chivalry wasn't dead by opening the door for me. He was now two for two. Being on time and now this. All he had to do was get a few more things right and I was his for the taken.

"Right this way," the hostess spoke and guided us as we entered the restaurant. We were seated in our seats that he had reserved for us earlier. The waitress then poured water into the glasses that were on the table and placed the pitcher in the middle of the table. "Here are your menus, your waitress will be right over."

"Thank you," I spoke for the both of us.

"You are gorgeous, Babygirl," he complimented just as the waitress walked off.

"Thank you," I replied, blushing hard.

"So, let's get to know each other better. Are you from here?"

"No, I'm actually from Louisiana. I've been in Texas for a few years though. My mom is dead, my dad was a pimp who moved me and the family around a lot. I moved here with my stepmother, one of his women whom he married to escape him some time ago. Eventually, he was able to locate us. He took her, and wasn't too concerned with me, so here I am." I shrugged my shoulders like what I'd said didn't faze me when in fact I was holding my breath, waiting to see what his response would be. I couldn't believe I'd just sat here and gave my life story to a man I hadn't known for 72 hours.

"Damn," he let out. "I wasn't expecting all that." Before I could respond, the waitress walked over and introduced herself.

"Hi, my name is Sasha and I'll be your waitress for the evening. Can I start you two off with any drinks?"

"We'll have a bottle of your finest wine and a shot of Patron for the lady," Christian ordered.

"Got it. I'll give you a few minutes to look over the menus and I'll be back to take your orders."

Once she was out of earshot, I spoke. "I'm sorry. I swear I didn't mean to divulge so much so soon. I'm usually a very private person."

He reached over the table and put his hand on mine. "You good, don't worry about it." He rubbed my hand softly and I felt my body heat up.

"Here we are," the waitress returned and sat the wine bottle down as well as the shot of Patron.

"We'll both have the sirloin dinner. A1 sauce on the side. Is that good for you, love?" Christian inquired, making the waitress smile at me.

"Yes, that's fine," I replied, in shock that he would order my favorite steak.

"Great, I'll take your menus." We handed her our menus and off she was again.

"Wow, how'd you know I loved sirloin steaks?"

"I didn't. I just guessed and I'm glad you are impressed by my choice." He winked at me, and I smiled.

"And why the shot of Patron?" I picked the shot up and held it in my hand.

"Because your response to my question was shocking and I feel like you need that shot after that one. Babygirl, I want to be a part of your world. You don't have to feel alone when I'm around, or even when I'm not. I'll make sure of that."

"Where are you from Christian?" I had to switch gears because if I didn't, I was sure to start getting emotional.

"I'm from Houston but I live here in Dallas. My parents are still together. I own a lot of real estate, a car lot, and I have my hands in other stuff," he divulged. I giggled a little because he had answered my question all in one sentence the way I'd done when he asked me. His life was the total opposite of mine.

"How old are you?"

"I'm old enough," I answered. He laughed and asked me again.

"Scriously, how old are you?"

"I'm twenty, but please don't let my age stop you from wanting me because I'm very mature."

"No way, you are legal, so we good." We both laughed.

After dinner, we went for a walk in downtown Dallas. Christian was very romantic; we talked about everything. He made me laugh and I loved that whole gangsta shit he had going on. I didn't ask him his relationship status, and at this point, I didn't know if it really mattered. All I did know was that I felt special in the moment.

We arrived back at my apartment, and instead of offering to walk me upstairs, he just got out and opened my door. I enjoyed a man who took charge and didn't have to be asked to do the simple things. He went in for a hug and held me tight. Those broad shoulders and strong arms made me feel secure. Pulling back from each other, I made the first move and kissed his lips. He accepted it, and we kissed passionately in front of my door. Once I was inside of my place with the door close, I leaned against the door and sighed a sigh of beautiful content.

Kicking off my shoes, I dropped my purse on the couch and sat down to savor the moment. Soon as I did that, Lily popped in my head. I wanted to walk over to her apartment but decided to call instead. The phone rang three times before she picked up.

"Bitch, where have you been?!" I spat angrily. "You got me blowing up ya phone like an ex you dodging or a bitch you owe money to. What's going on?"

"I'm so sorry," were the first words she spoke.

"Sorry for what Lily, the fact that you had me worried half to death or that you didn't care enough to reach out?"

"I tried to rob a man and he walked in and caught me." She spit out the words so quick, I almost missed what she said.

"Okay and why would you be sorry about that?"

"Because he took my bag, and all of the money I had for us to get a car was in it. He took it all." She cried.

"Lily, you really went MIA over some damn money. You could've come here and told me as soon as it happened. Your safety is more important to me than anything. I'm glad that you're okay. And you shouldn't be out there robbing people because you see how that shit can come back and bite you in the ass. I worry about you when you don't answer my phone calls. Don't let this happen again."

"Okay I won't," Lily told me.

"I'm still not happy that you lost all of that money and now we still have to catch cabs," I joked, and we both laughed.

"I know and I'm really sorry. I freaked out big time and went to stay at a hotel. Running from my problems because that's what I'm used to," she admitted.

"We can't keep living in the past, it'll make it harder for our future."

"You're right. So what about your new guy? I saw him leaving your apartment." She changed the subject.

"Girl, Christian is the man. He's everything I've been looking for. He doesn't make me feel uncomfortable about myself."

"I'm so happy, and this calls for a toast."

"Then why are we on this phone then... I'm on my way."

Making my way downstairs, I stumbled on a man sitting on the steps. The night breeze had him rubbing his arms in an attempt to get warm.

"Ma'am, do you have anything to eat?" He asked me.

"I'm sorry, sir, I don't, but here's a few dollars." I pulled a few ones out of my bra and handed them to him. Before walking away, I thought about how I used to be homeless, from room to room.

Wanting to help more, I went back to my apartment and grabbed soap, towels, deodorant, and blankets. I looked in the refrigerator and grabbed milk and water. Grabbing a few items from my pantry, I put all of the items in a big bag and carried them down to the man. When I made it back downstairs, I noticed he had a bowel movement and was still sitting there.

"I'm so sorry about the smell, I have a disorder. I go back and forth to the hospital trying to get it taken care of," he said to me.

"It's okay, sir. I'm not here to judge you." I gave him the items and walked away, making a mental note to bring him some more stuff later. He looked real familiar and I was sure I'd seen him around. I finally made it to Lily's apartment and made myself comfortable.

"What took you so long?" She asked.

"I had to stop and take care of something. It's taken care of now so let's turn up," I told her. We drank until we were both numb.

CHAPTER SIX

Babygirl

Friday night at Debo's was epic. Lily was turned up as usual and I of course was laid back, chilling in the cut. I made the decision that I wasn't gonna do too many private dances tonight. Being alone with those creepy ass men that came to watch us made my skin crawl after a while. Lily, on the other hand, was making her rounds. She was about her money for sure. Bobbing my head to the music, I heard my name called and turned to find Debo storming towards me with an irritated look on his face.

"There's someone outside looking for you," he let me know.

"Okayy," I dragged out, confused as to where the irritation was coming from.

"It's the same dude that's been stalking the club the last three weeks or so but ain't been spending no change. You need to see what that's about. This establishment is for spectators who spend money, Babygirl." Nodding my head, I went to do as he said.

I didn't know who it was that had been looking for me, but I was going to find out. I didn't want to be on Debo's radar if it wasn't in a positive way. When I made it outside, I swore my heart had stopped and my legs would no longer move. After five long years, my dad was standing before me, in the flesh. I wasn't too worried about what he'd do to me after all this time. I couldn't say that his visit didn't shake me up a bit though.

"Babygirl," he called out to me. The pitch in his tone told me he was excited, and I didn't know how to respond. "It's been too long. I've missed you all these years and needed to see your face. I retraced my steps to find you and here we are face to face," Jonathan said.

"Retracing your steps would have led you back to that filthy hotel that you dragged Alice from all those years ago," I spat angrily.

"I'm so sorry, please forgive me," he all but pleaded. "Please give me another chance to make things right with you. My world has been turned completely upside down. Alice left me about a year ago and I haven't seen her since. I have nobody, and nowhere to go."

The whole time he talked, the angrier I got. I was angry because my drinks were beginning to wear off and for some reason, my now sober heart was softening for my dad. Had he done me wrong my whole life? Hell yeah, but at the end of the day, he was still my dad and I had to suck it up and accept it for what it was. Finally, I gave in.

"Okay dad, you can come stay with me until you're back on your feet," I said hesitantly. I honestly didn't know what I was doing, other than what I thought was right. He hugged me tight and kept thanking me for being so gracious. "You're still my dad and I don't want to see you out on the streets just because I'm angry with you, that would be so selfish of me. I forgive you." When he pulled me in for another hug, the floodgates opened, and the tears poured from my eyes freely.

Just then, the club doors opened, and Lily walked out. Seeing my face full of tears, she immediately went into defense mode. I shook my head and held my hand up for her to chill. Pulling away from my dad, I introduced the two of them.

"Come to the back when you are finished here," Lily said before looking my dad up and down and walking off.

"Hey, let me grab my stuff and then we can head back to my place. I think it's best you wait out here though. The way you've been lurking around, my boss isn't a big fan of yours."

"I understand, Babygirl. I'll wait here for you."

I nodded my head and turned to head back into the club. I made my way through the crowd and back to the dressing room. Entering the room, I caught Lily stuffing that shit up her nose.

"Lily, I thought you told me you weren't into that anymore!" I snapped frustrated. Storming over to her, I pulled her seat back.

She looked up at me with a pitiful expression. "I have an addiction, Babygirl. I really need some help," she admitted.

"Would you be willing to check into a rehab?" I asked. If she really needed help her answer would be a no brainer.

"No no no, I'm not doing all of that."

"All of what? It's simple. I'll even go with you and help get you checked in. You will receive the help that you need." I could tell that she wasn't trying to hear me when she changed the subject.

"What is your dad doing here?" She questioned.

"So much for you wanting help." I rolled my eyes and went to my locker to pack up for the night. "And my dad is in a bad spot in his life. He needs me right now, that's all."

"Well shit, you just needed him years ago, remember," she spat.

"Yeah, I know, but two wrongs don't make a right; he's my dad."

"Uh, more like sperm donor," she mumbled. I ignored that comment. "But, you do what's best. Let me know if things go left and you need me. I'll be there with my boots on, ready to stomp something." We both chuckled and I shook my head.

"You'll be the first one I'll call." Throwing my bag on my arm, I gave her a hug. "Call me when you make it home and get rid of that shit before Debo catch you."

"I will." I gave a few of the girls waves as I made my way to the exit. When I made it back outside, my dad was waiting for me like he said he would be.

"Okay dad, let me call us a cab."

"A cab?" He questioned.

"Yes, a cab. I don't have a car right now, but I do have my own place and a job. It may not be the best job, but it pays the bills."

"Well, that's alright, Babygirl. I'm proud of you." I smiled inwardly at his statement. That was a first.

We didn't have to wait long for the cab after I called for it. The ride to my apartment was a quiet one, and it was a silence that was needed. Every now and then I peeked over at my dad and found him looking out the window. I wanted to know what was going through his head. I also wanted to pick his brain and ask the burning question in my head, what took yo ass so long to come for me? Figuring that I'd have time to do that since he'd be staying with me temporarily, I let it go for now.

When we got to my apartment, he seemed all over the place. His eyes darted all over the apartment and I took mental note of his actions. "I don't know what you're looking for, but you need to get some rest," I told him. "Here's some blankets and there's the sofa," I pointed. Once he was settled, I went to my room.

Checking my phone, I noticed I had three missed calls and eight texts from the same person, Christian. Christian had been calling and texting since 12AM. It was now three in the morning. I hurried and called him back. He answered on the first ring.

"Damn baby, I've been calling you," he let out as soon as the call connected.

"Yeah, I just looked at my phone. I had a lot going on tonight, including my dad showing up at the club," I told Christian.

"Wait, what? Your dad showed up at your job? Do I need to catch an early flight to come check that?" Christian was upset. He'd taken a trip out of town for business earlier in the week and we'd kept in contact on the daily.

"No baby, it's fine. He's gonna stay with me until he can find a better situation."

"You mean to tell me you bout to have a pimp living with you?"

"No, baby. He's not into that anymore," I lied, saying what I thought would make him feel better about the situation. "He just needs a little help."

"Don't ever make a decision like this again without talking to me about it first," Christian told me. I nodded my head as if he could see me. "Next time answer the phone for yah man too. I've been missing you like crazy, and I want to see you as soon as I land," he said.

"Okay it won't happen again and where would you like to meet?"

"Meet? No baby, I want you to come to my place. I got something special for you, too. I also need to talk to you about your job. You're with me now and I don't want my girl out showing her goods to nobody. We'll talk about it later though. I'll hit you when I land."

"Goodnight Christian," I said but he had already hung up. I was excited about seeing him later and happy about the surprise he had for me. He seemed a bit controlling now, a stark contrast from the Christian I had met three weeks ago. I brushed it off as him just wanting to make sure I was good, seeing as I did tell him about my dad abandoning me at one point. Putting any negative thoughts out of my mind, I went to sleep.

CHAPTER SEVEN

Babygirl

I got a few hours of sleep and woke up to my dad standing over me. I jumped at the sight of him. I wasn't used to a man living with me and thinking about my past scared me. For him to be standing over me was very uncomfortable. It had only been one night, and he'd been comfortable enough to tour my place and find my bedroom. He was lucky that he had a good reason in the form of scrambled eggs, butter grits, and toast served with jelly and a side of orange juice.

"Thanks, dad!" I said while taking the tray from him.

"Can we talk, Cameron?"

"Sure, go for it."

"I'm sorry for leaving you years ago. Although it's no excuse, I felt that the lifestyle I was living wasn't suitable for you and you were better off without me. I saw you in that closet hiding when I came to get Alice. I left you there on purpose and I was wrong. I just didn't want you to continue suffering from being around me anymore." His face was sincere and I felt his words were genuine.

"Listen dad, I forgive you. Yes, the mental and physical abuse I suffered at your hands still hurts me to think about to this day. Mom didn't protect me from you and for the longest, I hated the both of you. I cried many tears every night because I felt like my life was on hold. I didn't know how to let it go. I was angry all the time. I'm choosing to let that go because I want to move forward and be at peace. I love you dad and I'm here for you. My door is open to you as long as you need me." I poured my heart out to my dad and we both cried in each other's arms.

That moment was needed for the both of us. After finishing my food, I got dressed and we went shopping. I didn't have a lot of groceries at my apartment, and I knew he'd get hungry at some point while I was out at Christian's place. I let him load up with all of the groceries he wanted at Walmart to satisfy his appetite. I didn't know how long I would be at Christian's house, and I wanted to make sure he was straight. I also let him pick up a few under clothes as well as hygiene products.

As we shopped, a few people commented on how we looked just alike. I never got the chance to feel what it felt like to have a dad to do small things like this, so I was relished in the moment with him. He loved food just like me, so we made a quick stop at McDonald's once we left Walmart. Surprisingly, we ordered the same thing. I laughed once he realized it too.

Once our stomachs were full, we headed back to the house. Stepping out of the car with groceries in hand, I noticed Lily sitting out in front of the building with a random man.

"Hey," I greeted her.

She looked up at me and smiled. "Oh, hey girl."

"Hey," I repeated, "what you up to?"

"Oh, nothing. I'm just sitting out here enjoying myself with my boo," she replied.

I went to say something else but decided against it. She was acting a little weird and I'd told her time again about having random men around where we rested our heads. As prime dancers at a premiere club, I felt that we were targets for both me and women. No matter how many times I tried to drill that into Lily's head, she didn't get it. I started for the steps and took them one at a time with my dad trailing behind me.

"Okay dad, I'm going to put these groceries away real quick and whip up something before I head out. Now, I can't cook much, do you think a pot of spaghetti would be good for you?"

"Whatever you make is fine with me, Babygirl. Here, let me help." He walked with me into the kitchen, and we unpacked the bags together. Apart of me wanted to stop time just to be able to enjoy this moment for a longer period of time. This was how a normal father/daughter duo should be. "Do you need anything else?"

"No, dad, thank you. Go ahead and sit down while I whip up this spaghetti." He went back to the tv while I set out the ingredients for the meal. If someone would've told me that I would be able to be in the same room with my father and not want to spew a bunch of foul words at him for my upbringing, I would've laughed. I knew that mending our relationship would do the both of us some good.

I made the spaghetti in thirty minutes and set the pot to the side for him to have whenever he was ready. Checking the clock on the stove, I took note of the time and left the kitchen to make myself presentable for Christian. I couldn't wait to see my boo. I had been missing him terribly and it felt good to know that he'd been thinking about me too.

When I arrived at Christian's place, I was shocked to see how he was living. Now, I could tell he had some paper by the way he tossed it in the air at the club and the way he spent on me while we were out but judging by his home, I'd underestimated just how much he was working with. This man lived in a gated community that housed a few large homes, including his. From the end of the driveway, I could see the four-car garage that I was sure housed his car collection. Parked in front of the house were two cars, one being a monster truck. I was in awe.

The driver Christian had sent to pick me up, drove slowly up the driveway, giving me a chance to admire the well-manicured grass and the cobblestone driveway. I nodded my head up and down, giving compliments in my head.

"Do I get out or wait for him to come and get me?" I asked the driver.

"You can go ahead and knock on the door, he's expecting you," he told me. When I knocked, an older lady answered the door.

"Right this way," she told me, and I followed closely behind her. As we walked, I was amazed by the art that hung high up on the walls. The details were so intricate. I knew that someone other than Christian had decorated the house.

"Here you are." The lady opened the door to a beautifully decorated room. Inside, there was a table set up with fruit and wine and other assorted foods. I didn't waste any time grabbing a handful of grapes. I would wait until later to taste the wine. Just as I went to stuffing my face, Christian walked in.

"Well, hello, miss lady," he greeted me.

"Oh, hey baby." I smiled, trying to look cute with my mouth partially full.

"Are you comfortable, my love?"

"Oh, yes, I'm very comfortable," I responded while swallowing.

"Good. I have something for you, and I can't wait until after dinner. Come walk outside with me. He held his hand out for mine, and I grabbed his, walking outside anxiously. He escorted me to the backyard where a nicely decorated patio was set up for the evening. There was a big pool with a jacuzzi attached to it, and two chained pitbulls that began barking madly at my unfamiliar face.

"Aye!" Christian yelled out and the barking immediately ceased. "Close your eyes," he said to me. I closed my eyes and walked closely to him. "Okay, you can open 'em."

I opened my eyes and there sat on the side of the house a black-on-black Range Rover with a bow on it. How I missed it when I first pulled in was crazy. Still, I couldn't control my excitement.

"Baby, is this for me?!"

"It ain't for those damn pitbulls over there, " he joked. "No more cab hoppin'. I ride clean so my girl gotta ride clean too." I jumped up and down excitedly and threw my arms around his neck.

"Thank you, baby," I kissed his lips sensually. I was beyond appreciative. He let me go so that I could admire the car in all of its glory. It was decked out and I knew I must've looked like a kid, all giddy and shit. Kissing him again, I thanked him a few more times before we headed back to the patio. We sat on the patio and talked for a while, when the subject of me dancing came up.

"I don't want you dancing at the club anymore. You won't be going back there," he told me. I nodded my head in understanding of his direction. I didn't argue with him because he was right. He included that if I wanted to work, I could find a job that didn't involve me taking off my clothes. He expressed that he'd much rather me focus on going to school, but it was a decision I had to make.

As we talked, a man walked out with plates in his hands. Assuming it was dinner being served, I smiled in anticipation of what we were having. I watched as he set the plates on the table and pulled the lids covering them off, revealing baked chicken, green beans, and salad.

"This looks delicious," I told Christian as I dug in.

"I'm glad that you are enjoying yourself," Christian told me.

"I am, thanks babe. So, tell me about your real estate business, it must be doing well."

"Well, yes actually, it's doing really well and let's not forget the car lot I own too," he added.

"Oh yes you did mention the car lot, I forgot about that."

"Yeah. I have my hands in some other stuff but the less you know the better off you are, understood?" He smiled and put his hand over mine, giving it a subtle rub.

"Yes, I completely understand. I won't ask anything that I'm not ready to hear an answer to."

"No, it's not that I don't want you to know anything, it's just better off if you don't know certain stuff. I'm a gentleman with you but see in these streets, I'm a real gangsta. I dib and dab in things that could come back later and bite me in the ass," Christian explained.

"Okay bae," I simply replied. I wasn't naïve. I figured he was involved in the drug game and didn't want me to know. I could accept that. At least there wasn't any signs of him being a pimp in this big ass house.

"Don't worry yourself about what I do. Just know you straight and you won't have to want for anything else in life. You with me, you with a boss," he smirked. I smiled as he pinched my cheek, playfully. "So have you hooked up with any of these flunky ass men since you've been working at that club?" He asked.

"Oh no, I just dance, get my money, and get off the stage. I rarely do any private dances; I leave that to the other girls. I'm a virgin, Christian." I held my head down as I told him my truth.

"Damn, that's different. A virgin working at a strip club. I won't take you fast, and you don't have to do anything that you are not ready for. I be so busy chasin' money, my mind don't even be on pussy. I haven't got my dick wet in three months. I don't pass out dick," he made clear.

"Okay boss, I hear you. I'm sure you could have whoever you desire. You are a very attractive and successful man, and I am happy to have you," I said. We fell into a deep kiss that heated my body up a little.

Pulling back, he looked me in my eyes and told me he had my back no matter what. As sensitive as I was, it didn't take long before tears started to roll down my cheek. He planted soft kisses on the both of them. I'd never had someone to say the things that he had just said to me. And it felt good to hear them.

After dinner, he took me on a tour of his house. I couldn't help but comment on every picture that hung along the walls. We entered one of his five bedrooms and there sat an aquarium that was built inside the floor. The fish actually had their own room!

"I've never seen anything so stunning, Christian," I marveled.

"This belongs to you now, if you're willing to accept me. What do you say?"

"Well, I have to sort things out with my father first. You know he's living with me until he gets himself together."

"You don't have long to decide," he told me in an impatient way. I wasn't sure about moving in with Christian, he seemed very demanding. It was clear that he was trying to dictate my life.

"I'll talk to my dad tonight when I get home," I assured him.

"Tomorrow when you get home," he made clear.

Although skeptical, I agreed. "Yes, tomorrow when I get home. I will talk to him about any plans he may have."

"Good deal," he said, grabbing my hand to walk into the next room. He let me know that it was the master bedroom. The room was massive, with a king-sized bed, and three tv's that hung on the wall.

One was for watching shows and movies, one was for playing his favorite video games, and the last one was a video surveillance that flipped back and forth to different areas of the house and outside. Walking me to the closet, he opened it up and my eyes lit up at the designer items. It was filled with MK, Coach, Fendi, and more. I also took note of the jewelry collection. It was clear that this part of the closet was for a woman.

"All of this for me?" I asked.

"Yes, it's all for you, my baby," he confirmed.

"You're making me feel so special," I told him.

"That's because you are special to me, and don't you ever forget that."

Closing the closet door, we moved on to the next room, the game room. There was a built-in photo booth that I couldn't help but to pull him into to snap some funny pictures. He pressed a button, and it dialed his phone. He put his phone up to show me that our pictures were instantly uploaded from the photo booth to his phone.

"I'm having the best time. I can see us doing this a lot together," I gushed.

"Can you see a future with me?" He questioned.

"Right now, I'm just enjoying getting to know you," I told him honestly. From the way he looked at me, I could tell he didn't like my answer. "But I can tell you that you are the only man in my life who has my undivided attention," I quickly added. That was all it took for me to say before his frown turned into a smile.

For the rest of the night, we enjoyed each other's company. I played pool and drank a little while he smoked his blunt. Neither one of us were ready for the night to end. We took a shower together and I found out that he loved to sing in the shower just like me. Only his voice sounded better than mine. Getting out of the shower, he laid down before me, and I climbed in beside him falling into a peaceful sleep.

CHAPTER EIGHT

Babygirl

My overnight stay with Christian turned into a whole week. Finally making it home, I stepped out of my truck and Lily was sitting outside in front of the building. It wasn't like her to be sitting outside alone, so I concluded that she was waiting on me. After a beautiful night at Christian's, he gave me the key to the truck, allowing me to drive it home.

"Where you been bitch?" Lily asked as soon as my foot hit the ground as I stepped out of the truck.

"Girl, I was at Christian's house," I replied with a big smile.

"I see you smiling and shit, you must've had a good time. This yo' truck?"

"You know itttt!" I exclaimed.

"Jackpot!" She said, loudly. "Let's go for a ride." She went for the passenger door, and I stopped her.

"Not right now. I have to go inside and see wassup with my dad," I told her.

"I been outside all day and haven't seen him at all."

"Okay I will be down later," I told her as I walked up my stairs. I noticed the familiar faced homeless man sitting by the stairway. Remembering my trip to Walmart with my dad, I waved at the man.

"I have something for you. Give me one second," I told him. I hurried inside of my apartment to get the Walmart bags and came back out to the stairway where he sat. The bags were filled with snacks, drinks, and hygiene products. "That's for you, sir. I thought about you while I was out the other day."

"Thank you so much for being so kind. God bless you."

"It's my pleasure, sir." I shook his hand, not the least bit worried about where his hands may have been. Feeling good about my good deed, I went to walk back to my door and paused when I found Mrs. Thompson standing near my door with a worried expression on her face.

"Hey there, Babygirl," she spoke.

"Hi, Mrs. Thompson," I spoke back with confusion in my tone.

"Now, it's never my intention to be nosey, only concerned."

"Okay, is everything alright?"

"The guy that's been in your place, is he family?" She questioned with worried eyes.

"Oh, that's my dad." I breathed a sigh of relief, surely thinking that there was something big that was bothering her.

"I only asked because the other day while out walking my yorkie, it looked like he was removing some items from your apartment. Don't quote me on it though. You know these old eyes don't see that well these days."

Frowning up my face, I let what she said sink in. "Okay, thank you so much, Mrs. Thompson. I'll be sure to keep my eyes wide open," I told her.

"Okay, baby, and be careful coming in so late at night. Tthere's a man who has been sleeping by the stairway," she added.

"Yes, I know. He's my friend and he's harmless." Entering my apartment, my dad was on the sofa asleep.

When I'd come in to grab the bags, he wasn't there. He was somewhere in the apartment at the time though as he didn't just appear out of thin air. I looked at him with suspicion filled eyes and dialed Lily's number while walking to my room. I wanted to check for my gold necklaces and other antique pieces. I didn't want to believe my dad hadn't changed. I wanted Mrs. Thompson to be wrong, no, I needed her to be wrong.

"Hey wassup?" She answered.

"Have you noticed anything suspicious around my apartment lately?" I asked and commenced to a quick search of my room.

"No, I haven't. Why you ask? Is it because your dad is there, and you still don't trust him?" Lily questioned.

"Oh no it's nothing like that. I've been gone for a week, and you know you can't be too careful." I lied, opting out of telling her what Mrs.Thompson had told me. I couldn't tell her that I had a feeling my dad had betrayed me again. "But anyway, girl on to something else. Christian made me quit the club."

"What bitch?" Lily gasped. "So, you're not dancing anymore?"

"Nope, all of that is over with. I'm looking for a better job and he wants me to move in with him," I told her.

"That will be good for you friend. Just don't forget about me when you move and become bougie and stuff." We both laughed.

"You are my best friend, and I'll always be just a phone call away," I told Lily.

"Let's go for drinks later. Today makes six years since we've known each other," Lily said.

"Sounds good to me," I told her and we both hung up the phone. I called Christian next and he answered fast as hell.

"Hello, baby!"

"Hey bae, what are you doing?"

"Oh, chillin' over my podnuh's crib... about to get some shit going for today. Wassup, boo?"

"I think my dad has been stealing from me. Now, let's not get all out of control because I'm not exactly 100% yet," I told him.

"You gotta be fuckin' wit me, shawdy. That's it, pack your shit, you moving in with me today," he said with authority.

"I am. I just have to get him situated first." The words sounded crazy as they left my mouth. I wanted to get him situated but yet I thought he was stealing from me.

"Shid... let him have that apartment. That's a grown man, he will figure things out on his own. I'm worried about your safety so get out of there, NOW! I'll see you tonight."

"Tonight? I have plans with Lily."

"Plans? You still wanna hangout with the low class?" Christian fired back with a low blow.

"Low class? Come on now, Lily is my friend. The same low class who has been here with me since I was homeless. She has been my shoulder to cry on since day one, and my loyalty is all I know," I told him, not going for kicking Lily to the curb.

"You're right and any friend of yours is a friend of mine. She's welcome at our crib anytime if you trust her that much," he spoke, apologetically. Just like that, he'd switched up. I was beginning to think he was bipolar.

Later that night, Lily and I were dressed to impress. I had on a black and white Fendi catsuit with black heels. My hair was pulled up in a high ponytail and Lily had on a colorful maxi dress with some cute heels that made her dress pop. Her hair was in a messy bun. We swerved through traffic while Lily stood up in my sunroof living her best life.

I was enjoying my friend; happy that she was happy. We pulled up to Sally's sushi bar and used the valet to park my truck. We stepped out looking like a million bucks and all eyes were on us. Taking our seats, I ordered shots that we threw back like water. By the end of the night, we were loud and dancing to our own beat. I checked in with Christian briefly and zoned back out. After we calmed down and got ready to leave, Lily let me know that she didn't need a ride home because she had made plans with a guy she'd met to pick her up.

"Be careful, Lily," I told her and kissed her cheek. The valet pulled up with my truck and I headed back to my apartment with thoughts of detouring to Christian's place. I changed my mind, figuring that I could sleep in my own bed tonight seeing as I'd be moving soon.

Walking up to my apartment, I noticed the door ajar. I stopped short of going inside and had an internal battle with myself on whether I should go inside. Taking a deep breath, I decided I would go in. Yes, I was scared but still brave enough to go inside. My eyes grew wide at the sight of my once furnished apartment, emptied. I called Christian in a panic. This was a time where I actually hoped that he'd pulled one of his controlling stunts and came to get my stuff for me.

"Christian all of my stuff is gone. My apartment is completely empty. Did you come to move any of it?" I spoke as soon as the call connected.

"No, I haven't, and if yo' place is empty and you nor I have moved anything, then you need to get out of there," he told me. I complied and headed for the door while staying on the phone with him. Before walking out, I found a note in the doorway that I'd missed.

Dear Babygirl, I don't know how to tell you this, but I've become addicted to drugs so bad and in having no way to support my habit, I took a lot of your stuff to trade. When you make it home and see what has happened just know it was me and there wasn't any robbery, it was me. I have been taking from you and I am so sorry I hurt you again. You trusted me and I let you down again, I'm so sorry. I'm going to go work on myself and get some help. Please forgive me.

Love, Dad.

"Hello, are you there?!" Christian yelled into the phone.

"Yes, yes, I'm here, baby. I'm leaving the apartment and heading to you. I know who took my stuff, I'll tell you about it later." I quickly hung up. He'd done it to me again; he let me down. With a heavy heart and tears welled up in my eyes, I ran down the steps and into my truck. I hated him, I hated my dad so much.

CHAPTER NINE

Babygirl

When I woke up the next morning I was in Christian's arms. "Wake up, babe," I said to him. He rolled over and looked at the alarm clock on the bedside table.

"It's 5AM baby, what's up?" Christian asked.

"I never got the chance to tell you what happened last night. I was so mentally exhausted from all of that drama and fell asleep almost as soon as I got here. It was my dad that stole everything from me, there was no robbery," I told him.

"How do you know that?"

"My dad left me a note that I found as I was leaving out," I confirmed, sadly.

"You know that shit pisses me off right?" His voice went up an octave.

"Yes, Christian. I know, baby."

"And you know I will protect you with my life, right?"

"Yes, baby, I know."

"Where is he now?" He questioned, seemingly calm now.

"I honestly don't know, baby. He left my apartment before I got back," I admitted. He shook his head and got out of bed. "Where are you going?" I asked.

"I'm going to make you breakfast in bed since we're already up." He smiled his infectious smile, making me form one of my own. My phone vibrated just as he left the room.

"What's up Lily, it's 5:30 in the morning?" I answered.

"Your car wasn't home and it's late. I just wanted to make sure you were okay," Lily said.

"Oh, yeah girl, I'm okay. Something came up at my apartment when I got back. I left and came to Christian's house. I will tell you about it later." I still hadn't decided whether I wanted to tell her about what my father had done or not.

"Ok, well don't forget we have our gynecologist appointment this morning at 8AM," she reminded me.

"Damn, I'm glad you said something because I had completely forgotten."

"Okay because I don't wanna go alone." Her tone had changed, almost becoming childlike.

"Everything alright?"

"Yeah, I'm good."

"I don't believe that. Tell me what's going on, Lily." I couldn't help but to pry. Lily had something she wanted to get off her chest and the statement she'd made about not wanting to go to the doctor by herself spoke volumes. And that was because Lily usually did her own thing. She sighed and I could hear sniffling. "Lily?"

"I'm here," sniff. "The other night, I left the club with a guy and we stopped by the gas station to get gas. As he went inside to pay, I thought I'd be nice and pump the gas for him, so I got out behind him. When I went to pick up the nozzle, something was put over my head and I felt myself being lifted off my feet. I screamed, Babygirl, but no one came to my rescue. I was thrown into a car and we drove for a while. I had no idea where we were because I couldn't see but the ride was quiet with the exception of laughter every now and again. When the car stopped, I was yanked out and whatever was used to cover my face was snatched off." She paused and I held my breath. Sniff, sniff.

I shed a few tears of my own. "It's okay if you don't want to continue."

"I took note of where we were once I was able to see. It was the same area where I'd robbed that guy. He...he...he raped me." Her voice was slightly above a whisper. "I begged him to stop, and he wouldn't. I begged him, Babygirl."

"I'm so sorry. I'm sorry I wasn't there for you. Damn, why didn't you tell me sooner, Lily?!" I scolded her, not because I was mad but because I wasn't there to help her.

"No, it's my fault for being so careless. What if it was the guy that I'd robbed that set this whole thing up?"

Her guess didn't sound too far-fetched, but for some reason, I didn't want to tell her that. "I don't know, but I can't think about that right now. How have you been able to keep this from me? We were just together."

"I was still trying to process it, Babygirl. I wanted to believe it didn't happen. I tried reaching out to the guy that I'd been at the gas station with and I'm almost positive that he has me blocked. It just feels like my past is haunting me. I can't keep living this way, sleeping with man to man. I want to be happy like you. I want a man to come and sweep me off my feet and accept me as I am. I no longer want to walk around looking over my shoulder. I plan to repay everyone I've stolen from, especially dude that I robbed." Lily's repentance sounded genuine, but I was skeptical about the whole thing.

"That would be the right thing to do, but how would you get all of that money back?"

"I don't know yet, but I will find a way," she assured me.

"Okay we'll talk more when I see you in a few. Christian just walked into the room."

"Alright, I'll meet you at the doctor's office." Agreeing, we hung up at the same time.

"Who were you on the phone with?" Christian asked.

"That was Lily, bae."

"What y'all got to talk about this early in the morning?" He looked irritated.

"Christiannn," I dragged out his name, "we had an agreement," I reminded him.

"I know. We agreed that I wouldn't talk down on your friend and accept her and shit, but it's almost six in the morning, what y'all got to talk about that's so important at this hour?"

"Lily was raped!" I yelled a little.

"Raped? That bitch is a whole trick, practically giving her pussy away and now she hollering rape. She probably gave that man the green light on that pussy and forgot. And even if it was rape, why is she calling you like you supposed to come rescue her triflin' ass? I don't wanna hear anymore sob stories. Ya friend a thot, ain't nobody rape her lyin' ass." The malice in his tone let me know he meant every word he said. "Now, eat your breakfast."

"I think I've lost my appetite." Getting up from the bed, I headed towards the bathroom to take a shower. I brushed my teeth, showered, and put on a pink pair of Puma joggers, a black fitted t-shirt, and some pink and black Puma slides. I put my hair in a bun and applied light makeup to my face.

I felt bad about what Christian had just said about my friend. Sure, she was a free spirit who had no issue with sleeping with different men, but Lily was still a good person who didn't deserve to be raped. I knew she wouldn't lie about something so serious. Walking out of the bathroom, I walked past Christian whose head was in his phone and went over to my side of the bed to retrieve my phone and purse.

"Where you going? I know you not leaving because of what I said about ol' girl."

"I am offended by what you said about my friend, but that's not why I'm leaving. I have a doctor's appointment that I forgot about until she reminded me."

"Yeah, okay." Leaving him to think what he wanted to think, I headed out the door and to my truck. I texted Lily to let her know that I was coming to get her, so she didn't have to take a cab.

Arriving at Lily's apartment, I beeped the horn for her to come out. Looking up from my phone, I watched her sashay out in a red and white checkerboard dress and white sandals. Her hair was in a loose ponytail and as she got closer to the car, I noticed that she had no make-up own. The natural look suited her well. Getting in the car, we embraced each other, and as I went to pull off, a white BMW pulled up alongside of me and the window of the driver's side rolled down. The driver who I didn't recognize motioned for me to roll my window down too. Lily looked over at me and her facial expression showed that she was just as leery as me, but I rolled my window down anyway.

"Can I help you?" I spoke first.

"Hey, my name is Levi. I'm looking for someone and was hoping the two of you could help me."

"I'm not sure how we could help. Does the person you're looking for live in the building?" I don't know why I asked or even rolled my window down but what was done was done.

"Yes. What's your names if you don't mind me asking?" He was polite and seemed harmless.

"I'm Babygirl and this is Lily," I told him, and Lily hit my leg.

"Bitch are you crazy?" She said under her breath where only I could hear.

"Look, I have a man so if you're trying to hit on me, it's not going to work. Don't even waste your time." I switched up my attitude, quick.

"Naw ma, it's not even like that. I just came to say thank you."

"Thank you for what? Do I know you?" I asked.

He laughed lightly. "Let me refresh your memory. I'm the homeless man that sat right up on those stairs." He pointed at the steps. "You fed me and clothed me. You were the only person who stopped and helped me without judgment. Truth is, I'm a wealthy man and I grew up here in these same apartments. I decided to come back and visit by posing as a homeless person. I wanted to help those who would have a heart to help me during my time of need. Here, take this," he said while handing me an envelope through his window.

"No, I can't take that. I did those things out of the kindness of my heart." My eyes started to water.

"I'm also that same guy you met years ago at the hotel who told you to know yourself and your worth." His admission made goosebumps form on my arms.

"Wow, I remember that. I was out here about to do something I would later regret, and you stopped me."

"Yes, I did. Now take this check, and here's my card, you call me if you need anything." Without giving me time to protest, he drove off. I sat there for a while, stunned at how things had come full circle.

"Now that is crazy as hell. That man looked different with all that hair on his face." I said to Lily and wiped the tears from my eyes. Her face held a dead expression, and she rolled her eyes. Waving her off, I opened the envelope and a fifty-thousand-dollar check stared back at me. I put my hand over my mouth to muffle my scream. Lily held her hand out and I handed the check to her. Of course, I would share with her because she'd done the same for me. "We will cash the check tomorrow, let's hurry and get to our appointment before we're late."

We got to the clinic 10 minutes late. After giving the receptionist our names, we grabbed clipboards and pens and had a seat to fill the forms out. Lily was finished first, so she was called first. After a few minutes, I was called to the back.

"Hello, I'm Dr. Pam. I'll be doing your exam today." Dr. Pam checked my blood pressure, and I sat on the examination table.

"Will you be doing my pap smear?" I questioned, noticing the tools she pulled out.

"Oh no, we only do pap smears on Tuesdays and Fridays. I'll be drawing your blood and sending it to the lab for testing today." She drew my blood and told me I was all set to go. I walked out and Lily stood waiting for me with her discharge papers and a band aid on her arm from getting her blood drawn too. We both scheduled appointments to come back for our pap smears and left.

We hung out for the rest of the day, and she seemed to be doing better than what she sounded like on the phone earlier. Throughout the day, I checked my phone and couldn't believe Christian hadn't called or texted to check on me. Me and Lily grabbed a quick bite to eat, and I dropped her off home.

"Don't forget to pick me up tomorrow to go to the bank," she let me know as she stepped out of the car.

"Of course, I won't forget. I'll be here around ten iish," I confirmed and waited until she was in her apartment before pulling off and heading back to Christian's house. I missed him and I just hoped he was in a better mood.

CHAPTER TEN

Babygirl

The next day I was back at Lily's place to pick her up as promised. I'd brought the check Levi had given me and planned to stop at the bank after our run to the mall. Lily was too hype the whole way to the mall, she sang to the music on the radio, using her hand as a microphone. I was happy that she was able to be in good spirits after the traumatic experience she'd had. Entering the mall, the first store I wanted to hit was Saks. As we walked in that direction, my phone rang with an incoming call from Christian. I answered after the third ring.

"Where you at?" His greeting wasn't soft at all.

"I'm out with Lily shopping for a few things, wassup."

"I was just calling to check on you. And where you get money from?"

"Baby, Lily had extra money and offered to take me shopping," I lied. There was no way I would tell him that another man put money in my hands.

"You don't need her to do that. I'm your man, you with me now. You could've asked me for some money if you needed it."

"I know bae and I appreciate you having my back. I'll call you back in a few."

"Yeah okay, you just hurry home to me. I miss you so much," he expressed, lovingly. We hung up the phone and I went to catch up with Lily.

"Dang, Christian just won't let you out of his sight huh?" Lily joked.

"Nope, it's not like that. He just misses me when I'm away from him."

"Yeah, he's either clingy, controlling, or pussy whipped. I've encountered men that have been all three."

"Actually, I haven't had sex with him yet. I can only imagine how he'd act once I put this virgin pussy down on him." I rocked my hips back and forth and she laughed.

"I can't believe you haven't given up the goods yet." I could see her side eye, but it was true.

"I promise, I haven't. I'm waiting for the right time, and I've only been living with him a week or so. He hasn't tried to pressure me into it or even tried coming on to me. Now that I think about it, I'm wondering why he hasn't tried."

"Your guess is as good as mine. I know for sure he's attracted to you. Shit, he's been laying next to you for the last few nights."

"Girl I just want to give it up to him," I laughed. I was ready to have sex and who better than Christian to take my virginity.

Saks was packed, but I didn't mind. It felt good to spend money I didn't have to work for. I remembered the days when me and Lily would window shop, awaiting our time when we'd be able to show out in the stores. Although I had the freedom to indulge, I made sure not to spend too much, as I maintained a savings. It didn't matter that Christian was willing to give me whatever I wanted, I still saved for a rainy day.

We had so many bags when we left the store, we put them all in the truck and went to the bank. It was 3:54pm and we'd just made it to the bank in time before closing. There were only a few people inside and I hoped to be in and out. Lily decided to wait in the truck while I went inside to deposit the check in my account. While I waited on the line, I noticed Lily walking into the bank, what caught me off guard was the ski mask on her face and a black object at her side. She was a few feet away, so I couldn't make out what it was, and I prayed that it wasn't what I thought.

"Everybody get the fuck on the ground!" She demanded with authority. The lone security guard in the bank attempted to rush Lily, but she was too quick, spinning around and knocking him to the ground.

"What are you doing?!" I screamed, watching her, mortified.

"Shut the hell up!" She told me. I watched her pull something from her pocket and pull the security officer's arms behind his back to subdue him. As quick as she completed that task, she quickly jumped behind the counter and with a gun to the teller's head, demanding that she empty out the register. "Empty that trash can on the floor and put the money in the bag."

I wanted to close my eyes and believe this was all a dream. Right before my eyes, I watched Lily move like she had been planning this heist a while. She was calculating in her movements as she collected from the few registers that were open. My heart raced, thinking about the cameras the bank had that were sure to pick up our arrival and see that we'd come together. She was forever putting me in a fucked up position.

Now I knew why she was stalling to get here in the first place. The last few hours played in my head, and it all became clear. Back at the mall, I'd mentioned wanting to get to the bank before it closed, and she insisted that we had time. She was stalling for this moment here. Throwing the bag over her shoulder, she locked eyes with me for a split second before pointing the gun upward at an angle and shooting at the camera.

As she made her way to the door, the security guard was able to pry himself out of the restraint, raise his gun, and take a shot at her. He missed his shot, making Lily spin around and shoot back, hitting the guard in the chest. I couldn't look down; something told me he was dead. In shock, she stood there and stared at the man before making a mad dash for the door.

"Call 911, someone please call 911!" I yelled out in a panic once Lily was out the door. Seeing everyone in shock and not moving, I pulled my phone from my pocket to call myself. I reported the robbery and murder while trying to do CPR on the man although I knew he was gone. I cried so hard and looked around at the bank tellers that were both shaking and crying.

When the police arrived, we all gave our statements, mine with a twist. I never gave Lily's name and told them I didn't see the shooter. We were all made to stay put for a few until given clearance by the police to leave. Once I'd been given the go ahead, I left and went straight to Lily's apartment. I wanted to know what the hell she was thinking when she pulled this bullshit.

Furious, I banged on her door like a maniac. When she came to the door she was drinking wine and her eyes held an emotionless expression. Not asking permission to enter her place, I stormed inside. She slowly closed the door behind me and turned to face me.

"Lily, what the hell were you thinking? You just robbed a bank and killed the security guard."

"I know and I feel terrible about it." Her response had no feeling whatsoever. I wasn't convinced that she was sorry at all. "I didn't mean for it to go down like that. I just wanted to get the money and get out of there."

"Lily, are you fucking kidding me?! You robbed a bank and killed a man and that's all you have to say?"

"What did the cops ask you?" She disregarded what I said.

"You know what the cops asked me. And no, I didn't give your name if that's what you're getting at. I'm so mad with you right now, I don't even know how I'm looking at you. You may have successfully gotten yourself into something you can't get yourself out of. If those cops find out that it was you who robbed that bank and killed that guard, you are going to jail for a very long time. I just hope I don't get caught in the middle of this shit!"

"I just wanted to get this monkey off of my back, Babygirl. I have to repay some people. This shit has been haunting me," she expressed, and I couldn't show any sympathy.

"So, you decide to put yourself in a much worser situation than the one you're already in? That's about the dumbest shit you could've done."

"The cops will never know it was me. I shot out all the security cameras and the surveillance tape is taken care of."

"That doesn't mean anything. There are cameras all up and down that street," I reminded her.

"Stop panicking, everything will be okay," she stated.

"What makes you think the way that you do?" I asked, really wanting to know.

"How am I thinking?"

"You are thinking like a dumbass right now. You really aren't thinking about the magnitude of what's going on right now or what's about to happen," I told her. Lily popped her lips.

"It will be okay, no one will know. It's our little secret." I didn't like what she was hinting at, as if I was her accomplice.

Shaking my head, I decided it was time for me to go. With no further words, I walked out the door, leaving her standing there. Getting in my truck, I made my way to Christian's house. I picked up my phone for the first time since I'd dialed 911 at the bank and the screen showed multiple missed calls from Christian. Dialing his number back, I connected the phone to my truck's Bluetooth.

"Hey baby, I've been trying to call you," he said.

"I know bae. Something really bad happened today. I can't talk about it over the phone. I'll tell you when I get there," I told him.

"But you are okay, right?"

"Yes, I'm on my way." I hung up with him and focused on the road. I was trying hard not to speed, but I was anxious to get to him and fill him in on all that had gone down. As I drove, my stepmother popped in my head. I knew if I was able to speak to her, she would offer comforting words. I needed that in the worse way right about now.

Making it to Christian's house, I pulled into the long driveway. I could see him standing in the doorway of the house. As I went to park, he walked towards me. Turning off the ignition, I sighed and hung my head. Coming up on the driver's side, he opened my door and pulled me into him. I didn't know there was tears coming from my eyes until I felt them on my arm as I hugged him tightly.

"Tell me wassup, ma," he urged.

"Lily... Lily robbed a bank," I told him as I bust out in full blown no tears.

"I told you that hoe was bad news and you couldn't trust her. Why are you so upset tho?" He asked, pulling back from me slightly.

"Because bae, I was at the bank when she walked in and robbed the place and killed the security guard. I watched it all go down and when it was all over, I lied to the investigators." He hugged me again and told me everything would be okay and it sounded better coming from him than Lily.

"If this shit comes to our front door, Lily better be ready to take her lick or she will be dealt with," Christian stated with conviction.

"I just want to get in the shower and fall asleep in your arms," I told him. I didn't wanna think about today's events anymore, although I knew that would be easier said than done.

"Whatever makes you comfortable, baby." He took my hand in his and walked me inside the house. I felt safe, but I knew this was only the beginning of the bs ahead.

CHAPTER ELEVEN

Babygirl

The next morning Christian and I woke up to a hot breakfast. I'd tossed and turned all night thinking about yesterday's events and to say that I was nervous about what the outcome would be was an understatement. Christian thought it would be best to take me out to get my mind off of it. After breakfast, we had planned to go for a ride in the city. He had plans to take me horseback riding. As I got dressed, I noticed him admiring my body from where he lay on the bed.

"I want to see you," he said. With nothing but a bra and panties on, I slowly made my way over to his side of the bed. Without any words spoken, he reached out and ran the tips of his fingers across my skin from my breasts to my knees. The goosebumps that raised on my skin when he touched me was different. I held my breath as he leaned forward and kissed my stomach. The kisses then trailed from my stomach to the hem of my panties and down to my thighs. I shivered and couldn't help but to let a moan escape my lips. "I want you so bad, baby," he whispered.

"I want you too," I responded, giving him the okay to go further.

Grabbing me by my hips, he pulled me into the bed with him. He kissed me deeply and continued to explore my body with his hands. I felt him slowly dip his fingers in my panties to feel how wet I was for him, and my hips moved with his touch. His finger slipped inside of me, and my breathing got stuck in my throat.

"Damn baby, this the tightest pussy I've ever felt," Christian breathed heavily. I could hear him placing wet kisses on my panty line while pulling them off. Pushing my legs apart, he kissed me where I had never been kissed before.

"Oh Christian," I cried out at his tongue circled my clit. I bucked and squirmed and my moans grew louder.

Gripping the sheets, I cried out Christian's name as every part of my body seemed sensitive to the touch. I knew something was happening but I couldn't quite place the feeling as it had never happened before. He raised up and I could feel his hardness pressing between my thighs. He groaned as he pushed slowly inside of me and slid in and out of me. My own moans overshadowed his as I got louder. Christian started to get a little rougher when I dug my nails into his back. I was matching his pace, thrusting my hips upward to meet his.

"Oh, baby, something...somethings happening!" I yelled out. He thrusted harder and faster, making me buck wildly as I came. He moaned my name as his own orgasm put him over the edge. When were done making love and he removed the condom, he'd skillfully put on without me noticing, I felt wetness between my legs that was more than I thought it would be. Glancing down, I realized that the wetness wasn't only from the exotic love making we'd engaged in but also blood. "Christian, I'm bleeding!" I panicked.

He smiled. "That's normal ma, I popped your cherry. And that something you felt was you having an orgasm. Now, let's go take a shower." My legs were still in shock from having my first explosive orgasm, causing me to move slowly. After our shower, Christian lotioned my body and gave me a massage.

"This feels so good," I told him.

"I love you, baby," Christian let out. I was taken back by his profession of love for me. I paused for a second but finally replied that I loved him too. We stared at each other for a few minutes before I broke the stare. Fully lotioned, I got dressed and headed to the kitchen. My phone rang on the way there.

"Hello," I answered.

"Wassup chick, where you at?" Lily asked.

"Who is that?" Christian whispered from behind me.

"It's Lily," I whispered back with my hand covering the phone. "I'm at Christian's. Wassup?"

"Oh, nothing. I'm about to go cook something for my man. I was just checking on you," Lily said. I could tell that Lily was checking my temperature.

"How are you feeling?" I inquired, doing the same.

"I'm good girl, just like I was yesterday. I told you it will be okay; everything will be just fine. It was an unfortunate accident that can't be taken back." I didn't like her choice of words. It felt like she was trying to implicate me in her wrongdoing. Or maybe I was just paranoid, and rightfully so.

"So, what's your next move?"

"What do you mean, what's my next move?"

"Well, you know the cops will be on the prowl to find out who robbed that bank and killed that security guard." I pulled the phone from my ear and looked at it like it was a foreign object. Yeah, she was definitely acting strange.

"If the cops ask me..." before I could finish talking, Christian snatched the phone from my hand and hung it up.

"Don't discuss anything with that bitch over the phone! You don't know what the fuck she got going on!" Christian scolded me.

I nodded my head. "You're right, bae. Can you believe she's talking like I had something to do with what happen?"

"Exactly. That bitch is sneaky. You talking on the phone with her about what happen could likely incriminate you. Shit, she could flip it and put all this shit on you."

"You think Lily would do that to me?" The thought of it gave me an uneasy feeling in the pit of my stomach.

"Bae, you don't know what a person could do when they feel their back is against the wall. Someone was killed during the robbery, it's a whole different ball game now." His face showed concern.

"But it wasn't my fault!" I yelled out.

"I know that, and you know that baby, but you can't trust anyone outside of us at this point. You have to understand that once those investigators start their digging, your name will be associated with hers and you could go down for the robbery and murder along with her. Although you had nothing to do with it, the fact still remains that Lily got out of your car, went inside, and did the robbery. To top it off, when the people questioned you, you didn't give them shit, so if they see you on camera, it makes you look crazy. Them people know how to play the game when they need to. Fuck! This shit don't look good at all man." Christian's jaw tightened and I was still trying to wrap my head around this shit.

"So, what you saying is Lily will flip it on me so she won't go down?" I don't know why I kept asking questions I already knew the answer to. Somewhere in the back of my mind, I was hoping he'd put some type of doubt in my mind.

"That's exactly what I'm saying. So you have to use your head, play her close, but stop talking over the damn phone. Play her close enough to where you know where her head is at, but don't marinate around that bitch. For all we know she could be wired up. Come on, lets head out. I have a few errands to run before we go to the ranch."

"Okay." Maybe the ride with him would help me clear my head or at least formulate a plan as to how I was going to deal with Lily going forward.

Our first stop was the Waffle House. Christian parked in the far end of the parking lot and no sooner than he turned the ignition off, someone in a Jaguar pulled up alongside of us. I watched as the person and Christian rolled their windows down at the same time, made a quick exchange, and the Jaguar pulled off.

"What was that all about?" I questioned and he put his finger over his lips.

"Remember, don't ask any questions," he said. No sooner than we pulled off, I got another call from Lily. I looked down at the screen and debated on whether or not I should answer. "Go head and pick it up," Christian encouraged. "Remember, keep the conversation light and to a minimum."

"Hey, Lily, I'm kind of busy at the moment, can I give you a call back?"

"Yeah, sure. I called back to see if you were okay. The phone hung up on me earlier."

"Sorry about that, I didn't notice my battery was low, so the phone died," I lied, hoping she accepted it.

"No big deal. Hey, let's meet up later to discuss what happened the other day at the bank," Lily said.

"Sure, I'll hit you later for the details."

"Sounds good." I hurriedly ended the call, remembering what Christian had said.

CHAPTER TWELVE

Lily

"Is that enough probable cause to bring her in for questioning?" I asked the special investigator who was investigating the robbery and murder that happened at the bank. We both lay in my bed, butt ass naked, my fingertips making circles on his chest as he puffed a cigar. He nodded his head and smiled. Fucking him was my way of getting out of the charges that could be brought up against me.

"So baby, tell me what happened. I need all of the details in order to help you get ahead of this," the investigator said.

"Baby, there's not much else to tell. I don't want to be a part of this investigation in any capacity."

"I have to know the details, so I know how to go about flipping this on your friend," he pressed.

"All you need to know is that I walked inside of the bank, the bank was robbed, and the security guard was shot and killed."

"And the person who is responsible for this is your friend?"

"Yes, Cameron Jackson is her name," I told him. He nodded his head and got up from the bed. Scooping his clothes up from the floor, he began to redress himself.

"I'm going to take care of this, don't worry your little pretty self about anything." He kissed my lips softly and left out of my door.

I laid back on the bed and let out a sigh of relief. It felt good to know that my secret lover had my back and was willing to get dirty just to make sure that I was good. I still couldn't believe that I had actually pulled off the bank robbery. I mean, I was a little sloppy and didn't plan on things going so far like it had with the guard, but there was no way I could've predicted that that old man would've freed himself from those zip ties. I was just as shocked when he pulled out his gun and shot at me. When I planned this whole thing, it never crossed my mind that I would have to use my gun. I just wanted the people to take me seriously.

That morning before Babygirl picked me up to go to the mall, I had stopped by the bank. Decked in my all-black attire, including glasses and a bucket hat to shield my identity as best I could, I did a walk through without looking too suspicious. I'd even gone so far as to time how long it took for the tellers to complete a transaction. Feeling confident that I could make it happen, I went back home and waited for Babygirl. For the whole day of shopping, I let her swipe her card for all of my items. Shit, it was the least she could do for all that I'd been to her all these years. It was kind of like reparations for all the shit her father had put me through all those years ago.

I knew what I was conspiring to do to Babygirl was fucked up but she was just a means to an end. Although she was innocent, she would have to pay for what her father had done to me. There was no way around, over, or under it. And it was only the beginning of what I had in store for her. Shit was about to get real, fast. I had no time to feel bad for her. No one felt bad for me when I was in a fucked-up position, so I couldn't extend that same grace that wasn't extended to me. My phone rang next to me, and seeing Bobby's name on the screen, I answered.

"Hello."

"Hey, sweetheart. I need an address on your friend. I tried looking her up in the database, but it seems as though she's never been in trouble with the law."

"Umm, she lives with her new boyfriend, but I don't know where. Let me try calling her and see what I can get out of her."

"Okay, baby. Keep in mind that we are on a time constraint. I have to actively work this case."

"I know that Bobby," I snapped but quickly checked myself. I had to remember that he was helping me. "I'm sorry, baby. I'm a little anxious. Let me call Cameron and I'll get right back to you, okay." I made an attempt to smooth things over.

"I understand, love. No problem." He ended the call, and I dialed Babygirl's number. The phone rang a few times and just when I was about to hang up and call again, she answered.

"Wassup Lily?"

"Hey, you never mentioned the time for us to meet up or where we would be meeting. I could come to you." The phone went silent on the other end.

"Umm, no, that won't be necessary. And if it's okay with you, I'd like to hold off on the meeting today."

"Really? How come you're just now telling me? I could've had plans girl." Inside I was seething at her switching up, but I couldn't really show it.

"I know and I'm sorry. I've been moving around with Christian all day and I'm a little tired. Plus I feel a headache coming on."

"All the more reason for me to come to you. Come on, give me Christian's address and I'll take a cab there," I pushed. Babygirl was known to give in with a little peer pressure.

"Lily, you my girl, but I'm not giving you his address. This is his home and he's very private."

"Well, excuse me," I scoffed. "I thought it was your home too." Again, I was trying to reel her in, but she wouldn't bite.

"I'm not gonna go back and forth with you about it. Hey, I have an idea, Christian is having a kickback next weekend, how about we meet up do a little shopping and talk then?"

I thought about her offer and figured I could kill two birds with one stone. Christian had to have some balling ass friends. I could snag one and get in Babygirl's head some more. "That sounds perfect."

"Okay, are you cool to meet at the mall say around 12ish?"

"Damnnn, you can't come get a bitch?"

"I...."

"Girl, I'm just playing witchu." I laughed to lighten the mood. "The mall is cool. I'll see you tomorrow. Oh, and don't get too lost in that man. I've been there and let me just say it can get you into a world of trouble."

"Thanks for the advice. Here comes Christian, I gotta run." She ended the call, and I shook my head.

That man had her head gone and it was crazy to see. I knew Babygirl didn't know how to handle a man like Christian. I knew exactly what to do with a man of his caliber. Actually, I knew how to handle all men. I went to my text thread with Bobby and let him know that I still didn't have a location on Babygirl just yet, but I was getting close. His response was that I needed to get him a location like yesterday. I mentioned our mall trip, citing that he could pick her up there.

He quickly shut down my idea, stating that it would look too suspicious for him to pick her up while she was with me. Feeling frustrated, I left his message on read. I hadn't thought everything through to this moment. I needed a little more time to reel Babygirl in and convince her to help me cover up everything that happened. I knew it was the only way for me to make this work. Turning the ringer on my phone off, I laid back in bed to think. A plan would come together before I knew it. I'd come too far and had done too much to fail now.

CHAPTER THIRTEEN

Babygirl

"**B**aby, come in here and rub your man back," Christian called out to me. Tucking my phone in my pocket, I entered the room where he sat on the edge of the bed, looking at his phone. I liked the thug in him and after a long day in the streets, he deserved my full and undivided attention. I didn't mind massaging his back and catering to his needs.

Climbing in the bed behind him, I stood on my knees and began to knead my fingers into his back. "I invited Lily to your kickback, " I told him randomly, out of nowhere.

"Huh, what you do that for?" He turned to face me, making my hands drop from his back. "I told you that girl was foul. I don't want her around me or my people." The way Christian spoke of Lily made me think he had his own personal grudge against her. At first, I thought I was overthinking it and it was just his way of wanting to protect me, but it was becoming clear.

"Listen, I know that Lily is trying to set me up for that shit she did but I'm trying to go about figuring everything out the best way I know how," I reasoned. "We've been friends for years; I'm trying to give her the benefit of doubt."

"Now, you sound a little dumb and naïve. How can you know she's trying to set you up and still sit here and invite her to an event of mine? That shit gotta sound crazy to you. And it's clear that the time means nothing to her because if it did, she wouldn't be tryna set you up to take a fucking charge." His words pissed me off and I was fed up.

"Dammit Christian, I'm just so tired of you talking to me any kind of way. I need you the most right now and all you can seem to focus on is how you feel about Lily personally. In no way am I defending her, especially after what has recently transpired, but it seems to me that you have your own beef with her. I think we need to give each other some space. I have a lot going on and clearly you want me to move how you want and that's not working for me. You say you love me, and you got me, but it doesn't feel like it. I'm just gonna pack my things and go." I got up from the bed and was waiting for the moment that he would stop me, but he didn't.

"Are you finished?" He questioned with an uninterested look on his face.

"Am I finished?" I repeated.

"Yeah, are you finished talking out the side of your neck, " he stated firmly. I stood before him confused. "You are brave. Leave if you want to and you won't like the results." Still confused, I just stared at him. Standing up, he offered no additional words, walked around me, and out of the room. The look in his eyes told me he meant business and I dared not to test his gangsta.

I didn't know why things were going left with us. I needed someone to talk to, and knowing I couldn't call on Lily, I mustered up the courage to call the one person I knew I needed. Picking up my phone, I dialed a number that I'd still had committed to memory and waited anxiously as the phone ring. When the call connected, my heart leaped.

"Alice," I called out my stepmother's name.

"Oh, my dear, is this my sweet Babygirl?" She asked.

"Oh God yes," I cried. "I've been wanting to do this for years and..." I paused and sniffled. "I thought you forgot about me."

"Well, heavens no, I've never forgotten about you. I've waited years for this moment. I just knew that you'd find your way back to me or vice versa." The emotion was evident in her voice, she was crying too.

"Do you remember what you used to tell me growing up to keep me encouraged? About knowing my worth. I need to hear those words." The phone went silent, and I checked to see if she had hung up. Seeing that the call was still going, I just waited for her to speak.

"Know yourself and know your worth. Don't settle for less because if it's meant to be, it will be," she told me. I inhaled deeply and exhaled. I felt relaxed in my mind, body, and spirit after hearing those words. "What's going on?"

"Long story short, I met a guy who I'm falling for, but we've reached a rough patch already. We haven't been dating long and I've been picking up on red flags that are making me question my decision to let him in. I've even moved in with him against my better judgement, well also because of my father violating the sanctity of my home, but that's a story for another time."

"If your father has anything to do with it, I'm sure it is. Whatever it is, I'm glad you called and know that I'm here and we'll get through whatever it is together."

"You don't know how much that means to me. It feels so good to hear your voice, Alice."

"Aww, I'm here Babygirl. What else have you been up to?" For the next hour, I caught her up on everything that I had going on, leaving out the bank robbery of course. I didn't even tell her Lily's name, just that I had a friend who I became close with throughout the years. I also told her about the events that had taken place with my father. "Unfortunately, I'm not surprised at the events that took place with your father. I'm just sorry that you had to experience it. He's never going to change. I just hope for his sake that his past and present bullshit doesn't catch up to him and cost him his life."

I nodded my head in agreement. "I know." I could hear Christian making his way back to the room and quickly told Alice I'd call her back.

"Okay, I'll be here Babygirl. We've lost enough time; I wouldn't dare miss a call." Smiling, I promised to call back and disconnected the call.

"Babygirl," he laughed as he called my name. "What are you in here doing? You need to get up, put some clothes on, and cover that ashy ass face with some make-up," he spat, and I was stuck. The switch was so seamless. "You're not about to sit around the house and do nothing. Go read a book or something."

"What is your problem? Why are you talking to me like this?"

"Talking to you like what, '' he asked nonchalantly.

"Like I'm nothing to you. I can't be the woman you claim to love if you're talking to me like I'm some random in the street."

"Shit, I'm straight. Real shit, I was just downstairs thinking about this mess you've gotten yourself into. I knew it was something about yo friend I didn't like, and you wanted me to be open and friendly with her ass. I told you that hoe was bad news."

"I know what you told me Christian, but Lily was my friend way before I met you. And in all these years of knowing her, I would've never thought she was capable of no shit like this." I thought about her robbing one of her lovers a minute ago but reasoned that it was child's play compared to her robbing a bank and killing a man. "I don't know what else you want me to say about it. What I do know is that it's now affecting our relationship and making it a very unhealthy environment for me. I'm going through enough." I was in a vulnerable state, and he just couldn't seem to understand that.

"Man, fuck all of that. All I hear is more excuses you're making for her. It's the exact reason why she's been getting over on you for this long." He wasn't letting up.

"So, what are you saying, I'm naïve?"

"Now, you're getting it."

"Oh, you are something else. Yeah, we definitely need space because if you think that handling me this way is helping to sway me into thinking the way you're thinking, it's not. In fact, you know who you sound like?"

"Nope, but I'm sure you're gonna tell me," he said nonchalantly.

"You sound like my dad. The same man that you didn't want me around. The same man you didn't want me to live under the same roof with. You made me leave my home to move in with you and you have the same qualities as him." I went to turn and in seconds, Christian was in my face.

"I'm not sure when I made you think that it was okay to talk to me any kind of way, but you may wanna chill the fuck out! I don't know what you used to but I'm a man and expect to be treated as such. You got that?" I nodded my head and took a half step back, so we weren't nose to nose. I'd admit that his aggression scared me. "You over here trying to go toe to toe with me over a bitch that's tryna hang you out to dry while I'm over here tryna boss yo' life up. You got me fucked up, Babygirl, I know that's for damn sure." He walked around me and back out of the room.

A few seconds later I heard the front door slam, making me jump. Not only was my friendship with Lily on thin ice but so was my relationship with Christian. All of those small red flags had accumulated and here he was his true self. I had some things to figure out because there was no way I could continue on like this.

CHAPTER FOURTEEN

Babygirl

The next day, I was up bright and early, packing my bags. After Christian had left the house, I sat back and thought about my life and how things had changed in the blink of an eye after meeting him. That's not to say that it was perfect before he came along either, but it was my life and I lived on my terms. Since being with Christian, I had made quick and rash decisions to make him feel better about being with me. I could admit that now. I could also admit that I'd moved too fast.

With nowhere to go since I'd basically abandoned my apartment and didn't feel safe there after the shit my dad had pulled, I loaded my Range Rover and left out the house before Christian returned. I drove around in circles until I made up my mind to just go to Lily's apartment. Yeah, I was skeptical of being around her, and I could go to a hotel seeing as though I still had that check I never got to cash, but I opted not to. Although Lily was caught up in some shit, I had no reason to be scared of her like I now was of Christian. When I arrived at Lily's place, I spotted a tall, slim, bright looking man walking out of out of her apartment. I watched from the corner as he got into an unmarked vehicle that I instantly knew was a cop car.

"What is this girl up to?" I said out loud. In my head, whatever it was, it wasn't good because Lily hated cops. Just as I was about to continue driving up the street, she walked out of her apartment in a robe and over to his car. I could see him roll the window down and she ducked her head in. It didn't take a rocket science to know they were kissing. Hmph, was Lily having a secret relationship with a cop that she didn't feel I needed to know about?

It was one burning question that I wanted the answer to. I waited until the car pulled off, parked my truck, and hopped out on her before she could reenter her apartment.

"Uh, huh," I said loudly, making her spin around fast.

"Dammit you scared me, don't do that again," she let out while looking around me.

She made me do the same to ensure no one was behind me. "I was playing dang. What are you looking for?"

"Oh, nobody," she replied, pushing her door open. "I just haven't been feeling myself ever since the bank situation." I walked in behind her, closing and locking the door behind me.

"Yeah, same here but we can't live thinking about that every day. We have to keep moving as if nothing happened. If not, we'll stress ourselves half to death."

"You are absolutely right Cameron. It's over with now and none of it was my fault."

I paused, confused as to why she would be calling me by my government name. I was shocked because it was something she never did. "Cameron? Why did you just call me Cameron?" I asked, suspiciously.

"I just wanted to call my best friend by her real name," she responded, and it sounded weird when she said it. "I know it sounds crazy to hear me say it, huh?" She laughed and I gave her a small smile.

"Yeah, very crazy. So, who was that guy outside when I pulled up?" Her eyes darted around, looking at everything but me. "Lily, girl, what is wrong with you?"

"Nothing, and he's nobody important. Just an old fling that I hang with from time to time. He wasn't outside for long, when did you get to see him?"

"Well, I didn't really see his face, but I was turning the corner when I saw him getting into his car. As he pulled off, I was parking my truck. Since when we started keeping secrets from each other?" I tried to get information from her.

"I wouldn't call him a secret. I just never mentioned him. He comes by every now and then for an exclusive session. He loves the way I perform." She winked her eye at me and smirked.

"Hmph, it's one in the same."

"Girl, you haven't seen majority of the men I've had in the past. Trust me, this one is no different." She tried to downplay it but something in me knew better.

"I guess."

"What brings you by though? You didn't call or nothing. I figured you'd be laid up with your man. You know the two of you are two peas in a pod." I took a seat on the couch in the living room while she went into the kitchen. She returned with a tray of wine, cheese, and crackers.

"Since when did you get so fancy?" I asked, picking up a piece of cheese and taking a bite.

"I entertain according to the company I have. The guy that just left just so happens to like wine, cheese, and slow R&B."

"I see."

"Back to the reason you popped up."

"Right. Christian and I are having some issues and we're not seeing eye to eye. He's starting to remind me too much of my dad."

"Really, how so?" She questioned and I checked her face for sincerity. Feeling that she was, I went on.

"Ultimately, I just moved too fast. We hadn't been together long enough for me to take such a big step. Like we needed to get to know each other more, you know. Now, it feels like he's trying to control my movements, from how I look, where I work, and who I associate with." I tried not to make any facial expression when I mentioned who I associated with.

"Girl, I know yo' man don't like me. That's why you don't want me to know where he lives. It's cool though, I know I'm not everyone's cup of tea. As far as him trying to control you, that's what men do, but that doesn't mean you have to accept it. You know I'm here for you though just as you've been for me."

"I appreciate that. I'll only need a few days to get some things figured out."

"You take all the time you need. You know where everything is." She downed the rest of her wine, got up, and headed back to the kitchen. "Dang, I sho was looking forward to hanging out with you at that big ass mansion Christian lives in, Cameron!" She yelled from the kitchen. There she was again, calling me by my government. Again, I shook it off.

"Yep, that would have been fun. And this break I'm taking is not to say that we may not come back to each other. I need this time to figure out exactly what I want though. Fuck that kickback I invited you to, we can go out and have our own fun." If I had to convince myself that I was okay, then so be it. Anything was better than walking around feeling sorry for the decisions I'd made. Lily was down for going out as always and she still worked at Debo's. I hadn't been there since I quit so when she suggested we go there later tonight, I was down. "So, how have things been going with you and getting that monkey off your back?"

"Huh?" She questioned, returning back to the livingroom with her wine glass full.

"You said you were working on getting that monkey off your back, you were talking about your habit, right?"

"Oh, yeah, that. I'm still working on it. It's not an overnight thing."

"I see. And what about the money you're supposed to pay back?"

"I'm taking care of all of that. I gotta take care of me first though. And speaking of taking care, I have to give you your cut." She went to stand, and I stopped her with my hand out.

"My cut? Lily, I don't want anything to do with that money." She was tripping, and as much as it burned me not to accept it, I couldn't take anymore dirty money from her. I had to draw the line somewhere.

"Yes, Cameron, your cut. You earned your part of this money."

"Okay, seriously, stop calling me that. And I didn't earn anything."

"So, you put your life on the line and lied to them police for nothing? Girl, let me give you what you're owed."

"Lily, I don't want any of that money and that's final. And I would appreciate it if you stopped trying to force it on me."

"Okay." She threw her hands up in the air, signaling that she was backing off. "No problem at all. I'll be in my room. I'm gonna chill out until later tonight when we go out. Do you need anything?"

"No, I'm fine, thanks." She nodded her head and walked off. All the signs that Lily was tryna pull one over on me were right there in my face, but something in me was still holding out to the hope that she wasn't as grimy as she made herself out to be. I mean, we were like family. Then again, the word family was often thrown around so loosely and it was usually them to stab you in the back.

Night had fallen and I'd been lounging around Lily's house for most of the day, watching tv and drinking wine. She hadn't come out of her room other than to go to the bathroom the last few hours. Any other time, I would've taken it personal, but I appreciated being alone. Sitting back and thinking about my life, something in me said I needed to make a drastic change because the way things were headed right now, I didn't see a good outcome. With my mind in overdrive, I remembered that I didn't call Alice back yesterday. Grabbing my phone from my bag on the coffee table, I dialed her number. The phone ring twice before she answered.

"Babygirl?"

"Yes, it's me. Sorry I'm just getting back to you."

"Oh, no worries. I figured with all that we talked about; you may have been putting some things in order for yourself."

"You know me so well. I'm here at my friend's house for a little bit to clear my head. I think it's time for a change of scenery though."

"Babygirl." I heard Lily call out my name at the same time I heard a beeping sound on the other end of the phone.

"Babygirl, I have to take this call. I'll give you a call sometime later today or you can shoot me a text."

"Okay, no problem. I'll text you." She ended the call, and I went to respond to Lily as she made her way out to the front where I was. "Hey, you called me? I was on the phone with my stepmother."

"Who, Alice?"

"Yeah."

"That's so good. What did she say?"

"Not much, I built my nerves up to call and check on her. We talked like we'd never been apart. It felt good to hear encouraging words from someone I know I've never had to question. She's always been in my corner since I was a child and even for the gap of time when we didn't have each other, I always knew in the back of my mind that she was somewhere looking for me."

"Well shit, it's a good thing I have tough skin because you just made me feel like chopped liver. I do care about you, ya know."

"You know what I mean, Lily." I did my best to try and soften the blow without actually changing my statement.

"Yeah, I get it." She didn't sound convincing but decided not to expound on it. "I'm happy that you were able to reconnect with her though. Do you know where she is now?"

"Shoot, no. I didn't even ask, but I'll be sure to when I call her tomorrow."

"Cool, now let's go shopping. I'm so tired of sitting in this house bored," Lily said anxiously. "I'm gonna go throw something on." And here she was again ready to spend some money that she didn't earn with me right at her side.

Finding a parking space at the mall was always hard on a Friday evening. We had to be in and out because Lily had to work tonight. Finally finding a space in the second level parking lot, I parked and got out. My phone vibrated in my bag, and I pulled it out to check it. Seeing a couple messages from Christian, I shook my head and ignored them. I wasn't ready to talk yet.

Our mall trip lasted all of an hour and a half, with Lily doing most of the shopping and me picking up a few things here and there. As we exited the last store, Lily grabbed my arm and went to dragging me all through the mall like a maniac.

"Lily, what the hell? Girl you gonna make me fall," I complained as she dragged me until we made it to the parking lot. Once we got to my truck, I snatched my arm back from her. I went to say something to her when I spotted a man a few feet away watching us. He had to be about 5'9, he had caramel skin, deep waves, tattoos in his face, and a body that looked like he had done a 10-year bid.

"Get in the car," she demanded with base in her tone. Her eyes were wide and that scared me, so I got in on the passenger side since she'd already made herself comfortable in the driver's seat.

"We're we rushing out of the mall because of that man?" I inquired.

"It's Calvin Sims," she said as she drove my Rover like a race car.

"Calvin Sims?" I questioned, not having the slightest clue who the man was.

"Long story and I don't want to talk about it." She spoke with finality. And here I was, sitting in the passenger seat of my own vehicle without knowing what the hell was going on. Lost in Lily's shit again.

CHAPTER FIFTEEN

Babygirl

The weekend had gone by fast, and I felt like I'd turned up enough on Friday and Saturday, I didn't have any more turn up left in me. It was around one in the afternoon when I rolled over on Sunday and received a call from Alice.

"Hey, Alice, I'm so happy that you called. I was going to call you today. How are you?" I asked.

"I'm doing great, I just needed to hear your voice. It's been a couple days since we last spoke."

"You know, you can call me anytime and if I don't answer, I will call you back."

"I'll keep that in mind. You know we're just reconnecting, so I don't wanna intrude on your life or take up too much of your time."

"You're fine, Alice. I meant to ask you during our last two conversations, where are you living now?"

"Hot Georgia, sweetheart, and I love it. Where are you?"

"I'm still in Dallas. How long have you been in Georgia?"

"A few years now. I left your father in Tennessee and moved here with no regrets. That's where he hauled me off too when he dragged me out of Texas kicking and screaming. I still can't believe he came back to Texas, found you, and still didn't act right. I'm sorry about that."

"Yeah, and to think that I felt bad for him and gave him a place to lay his head when I thought he needed me. Only for him to rob me of the shit I worked hard for."

"Your father could be very manipulative, but we won't waste much time discussing him. I got away and moved to Georgia, and I have my own home. I'm rebuilding my life and restoring what has been missing. I plan to pay in full for this three bedroom, two bath home that I live in once I graduate medical school and become a registered nurse." I sat on the other end of the phone, smiling and enjoying my stepmother talk about her accomplishments. With all that my dad had put her through, she made it out.

"When's your graduation?"

"Next month actually and I would like for you to come out and help me celebrate. I'll buy the plane ticket."

"Oh no, I will pay for my ticket. You just walk across that stage with your head held high, knowing you made it," I told her.

"Thank you, darling. I'll be sure to email you the invitation soon as we hang up. I can't wait to see my grown girl."

"Oh, what I wouldn't do to be a child again these days. Under better circumstances of course."

"I wish it could've been better too. While we're on that subject, I want to formally apologize for leaving you all those years ago at that hotel. I never told your dad that you were inside, and I know it sounds bad, but I figured you'd be better off in a way. I had nothing to really offer you other than love. I really couldn't protect you from the coldness of your father because I was seeking protection myself. Know that I thought about you every day and prayed for your safety."

I teared up at her heartfelt words. "I figured someone had to had been praying for me because I've gotten this far. I'm just so thankful I was able to contact you. Thank you for never switching up on me and loving me as your own."

"You are mine, Babygirl, and I will always love you, nothing will ever change that. I made you that promise many years ago. I feel some tears coming on, so let's switch gears." She laughed lightly. "Tell me about this friend you met and got close to. You never told me her name."

"Oh, I met Lily at the hotel the next night after you left. She was just as lost as me and we had that in common. We clicked and had each other's backs from there. We struggled to take care of ourselves for the most part until we started dancing at Debo's." I cringed a little at how she may have viewed me now.

"Dancing?" Alice reiterated.

"Yes. I used to dance until I met Christian, and he made me stop. Around that time, he was such a gentleman to me. I thought that he wanted me to stop because he didn't want me in that kind of environment. You know, as a way of protecting me. In hindsight, I now know that it was the first step in his control. I moved out of my apartment because of him too. Things changed drastically and honestly, I'm hoping that this time apart will make him see the error of his ways and we come back together better than before." It sounded crazy after all Christian had showed me, but I had to be honest with the fact that I was hopeful for us to reconnect because I did care about him.

"Space is needed when there's constant commotion between you and your spouse, so you took the necessary approach. Has he called you?" Alice said.

"Yes, but I ignored his calls."

"How long has it been since you last talked to him?"

"About three days ago when I left his house."

"It's time to talk to that man to see where his head is at. Now, listen, I'm not telling you to be a fool for him. All I'm saying is know how to pick your battles and to know when they are worth fighting for. Now, go think about everything that we have talked about, and we will talk again soon. I have to go and study for my exam I have in two days."

"Okay. I love you."

"I love you too and be on the lookout for that email."

When I hung up with Alice, I started thinking about my own education. I grabbed my laptop and began researching how to get my G.E.D. When I typed it in Google, I learned that it was now called

Hiset and that there was a testing center right by Christian's house. My mind was made up, I would stay with Lily and focus on taking my Hiset. I would encourage Lily to take the test also. She needed to do something with her life other than robbing people.

"Hey, what you up to?" Lily asked, entering the livingroom that had become my room over the past couple of days.

"Hey," I looked up from the laptop. "I'm looking up some information on the Hiset test."

"What's Hiset?" She sat at the end of the couch I was occupying.

"It's the new name for the G.E.D test."

"Oh, okay. I see you girl, tryna get your education and shit."

"Yeah, I figured we could do it together." My phone rang and I picked it up. It was Christian calling and after having the conversation with Alice, I figured I'd answer.

"What Christian?" I answered and Lily got up to excuse herself.

"Baby, just give me a second to explain to you how much I adore you and appreciate you," he pleaded.

"You should've have thought about how much you loved and adored me when you threatened me and treated me like I meant nothing to you."

"And I'll admit that I was dead wrong for that. I love you, Cameron, and it hurts that we've been arguing the way we have been. I've never had a woman as selfless as you and I'm sorry for the shit I said. I was out of line, please forgive me." I felt the sincerity in his apology, but deep down, I also felt like he just wanted me back so no one else would take his place. It was a control thing for him. I couldn't make it easy for him.

"I hear you Christian and I want for us to be together, I just need space right now. I need time to think things over and to not make any mistakes. Just respect my mind and we will talk in a few days," I assured him.

"You mean to tell me I have to wait for you to make the decision? What about how I feel?" He argued.

"Christian, just because you decide that now you're sorry doesn't mean I'm rushing back to you. You did me wrong, so I get to decide the timeline on that. Plus, I'm working on something right now and I don't need the distraction," I told him. I disconnected the call before he could get another word in.

"Yo', what Christian was talking about?" Lily reappeared as soon as I sat my phone back down.

"Girl nothing that's worth discussing. What we need to do is discuss this test and you taking it with me." I pat the seat next to the couch and her face frowned up.

"Ummm, that's gonna have to wait. I have to run out for a few. I'm dancing tonight, but we can talk about it tomorrow."

"Okay," I replied, unenthusiastically. I wouldn't hold my breath waiting for Lily to want more out of life. Right now, I had to be selfish about mine.

CHAPTER SIXTEEN

Lily

Lily: You remember what we discussed. Well, it's time for you to prove your love for me. We have no room for fuck ups. I will contact you tonight at 11pm.

I texted Bobby from my phone as I sat in the club's dressing room. I really didn't have to come in tonight, I just said that to Babygirl so that I could shake her for the evening. I was really at the club for an alibi and to meet with Calvin. Calvin Sims was my ex and also the man I'd taking that money from a while ago. He'd been trying to track me down for a while now and for the most part I was able to evade him, that was until I saw him at the mall when I was out with Babygirl. I almost yanked her arm off trying to pull her out of the store.

I don't know why I thought that I'd be able to dodge him for long after owing him a nice piece of change. He'd popped up at the club the night me and Babygirl went out and once again, I made Babygirl leave a place, not caring that she wasn't ready to go. I let her know that Calvin was in the building, and I wasn't comfortable sharing space with him. I still hadn't told her how why or who he actually was. I needed Calvin dead though because I had no intentions on paying him back a dime of the money I'd taken. I definitely wasn't given him anything from the bank robbery.

Snorting another line of coke, I held my head back to take it all in, wiped my nose, and got up to head back out front. I'd texted Calvin to meet me with the promise of arranging how I was going to get him his money back. Little did he know, I had other plans for him, and he wouldn't need money for where he was about to go. I tucked my phone in my bra and walked slowly in my heels, spotting Calvin at a booth in a dimly lit corner of the club.

"So wassup, you got that for me?" Calvin questioned with his signature menacing look.

"I do Calvin, let me pull out the couple G's I owe you," I said slickly. "Where am I gonna have that kind of money on my person, do you not see how I'm dressed?" I motioned to myself, scantily clad in a two-piece bikini that left little to the imagination. I sat down next to him and put my hand on his thigh. He quickly removed it, throwing my hand in my own lap.

"You think this is a fucking game?" He whispered harshly through tight lips. "Where is my fucking money, Lily?" He gripped my thigh, squeezing it tightly.

I winced and spoke. "I can meet you with it tonight at Sam's Park. Ooouchh, please let my leg go."

"Listen bitch, I'm going to be at Sam's Park tonight. If you don't have my money, I'm gonna put a bullet in that empty ass skull of yours, do you understand me?" I nodded my head.

"I understand."

"For your sake, I hope you do." He let my thigh go, gave it two slaps, and got up to leave. I was shook and even more convinced that he had to go. I pulled out my phone to text Bobby and saw that he'd responded to my initial message.

B: Anything for you, queen.

I smiled openly and responded with the location of where we'd be meeting. I'd told Bobby all about my relationship with Calvin and even embellished the story a bit to work in my favor to make him hate Calvin even more. I knew it would be his pleasure to knock off Calvin for me. Bobby was the man who wanted to do anything to make me happy and he wasn't above killing for me.

Later that night, I sat in the car alongside Bobby dressed in all black, waiting for Calvin to arrive. I'd texted him with the time and we arrived thirty minutes earlier at Bobby's request. He wanted to check out the area before Calvin got there to make sure that I wasn't being set up. I was glad that his detective instincts were always on.

"Okay, baby, he just texted me and said he's about to pull up in five minutes. Are you ready?" Bobby was silent, staring out the window of his car. "Bobby," I called out to him while tapping his shoulder.

"Yeah?" He turned his head to face me.

"You good?"

"Yes, sweetheart. I just prefer to sit in silence when it comes to things like this."

"Oh, okay. I told him to meet me in the park by the court. You think we should head over there now?"

"We? There's no we, Lily. You stay in the car, and I'll go over myself."

"But, if he doesn't see me, he's going to know something's up." I didn't understand his logic about me not actually being the one to hand off the duffle bag filled with telephone books that I'd disguised as money.

"Tell him that you're going to set the money near the entrance of the court. I'll take care of everything else." He went to get out the car and I started to say something, but he shut me down. "Stay here, Lily."

"Alright," I replied with a hint of attitude. I was supposed to be running this show. I watched him walk off into the night and texted Calvin what he said. Calvin responded that he was two minutes out and that I'd better not be playing with him. I wanted to respond, "go to hell," but decided against it.

I waited in the car anxiously. We'd parked on the other side of the park out of sight from the courts, so I had no idea what was going on. Just as I went to text Bobby to see if Calvin had pulled up, I heard two gunshots. POW POW! They were loud, even in the distance. I sat up straight in my seat and watched as Bobby casually walked over to the car and got in.

"Done deal," he said once he was inside. "Grab that handkerchief out of the glove compartment." I did as he requested and watched as he wiped off the gun and put it under his seat.

"Are you okay?"

"Yeah, I'm okay. You know I will do anything for you, right?" Bobby said as he stared right into my eyes. I half smiled and nodded my head.

"I do. Now, let me give you something just to show you how much I appreciate what you've done for me." I reached over to recline his seat back and pleased him with only a technique that I had perfected. My baby had done his good deed and I was proud. One problem down, one more to go.

CHAPTER SEVENTEEN

Babygirl

"Flight 1025 going to Atlanta, GA, please get ready to board the plane." My flight was announced, and I stood up with my luggage. I walked in my stiletto heels towards the gate where my flight was boarding, and excitement filled my body. I was headed to see Alice. Today was her graduation ceremony and I would be arriving a few hours before. Getting comfortable in my seat, I pulled out the GED book I'd picked up before my flight and cracked it open to do some studying.

I was serious about my new journey and had come to terms with doing it alone. I was fine with it and concluded that it was for the best. Lily and I were on different paths and had been for a while and I was finally accepting that although we were friends, it was okay to move on without her when it came to this part of my life. The flight was a quick one. Once I made it off the plane, I grabbed my luggage and searched the crowd of people waiting for their loved ones, looking for Alice. I spotted her beautiful face as she briskly walked towards me with tears in her eyes.

Tears immediately filled my own eyes as she had gotten closer. We embraced each other with tight hugs that made me feel bubbly inside. Alice looked nice, toned, and fit, like she worked out every day.

"Oh my, it feels so good to finally be back in each other's presence. It's been a long time," Alice reminded me. I smiled and just stared into her beautiful eyes. "You have grown into a mature young lady. I can't believe this; I have waited so long for this moment."

"I've missed you so much. Ughh, I knew that before I got here, but now that I'm in your presence, that feeling is only amplified."

"Awww, my girl." She pulled me in for another hug. "Let's get out of here and grab a quick bite to eat."

"And we can go shopping. I remember you mentioning that you were indecisive about what you wanted to wear to your graduation."

"You're right. Let's do that and we can grab something at the food court." We walked out of the airport hand in hand and a part of me felt like a little girl again.

"Next we have Alice Cooper-Jackson!" Everyone stood up as they clapped for Alice. I was excited, as I cheered for my stepmother who walked across the stage proudly to accept her degree.

"You did it Alice!" I yelled from my seat. I smiled from ear to ear because I knew one day that would be me. "I'm so proud of you," I told her as we approached each other after the ceremony.

"Thank you." She hugged me and kissed my cheek. "Now let's go get something to eat and talk." I followed her to her vehicle, still excited about what I had just witnessed. It gave me the motivation I needed.

"You know what... there's something I've always wanted to tell you," Alice said while focusing on the road.

"What's that?" I asked.

"Well, do you know one of the reasons I've always been attached to you?"

"Because you love me so very much, " I said jokingly. Alice smiled.

"Yes, that's part of the reason, but also because you are the daughter that I never could have."

"What do you mean by that?" My smile had dropped.

"I never could have children with your father. I tried many times over the years and didn't succeed," she responded sadly.

"I'm so sorry to hear that. Did you ever go to see a doctor to see what was going on with your body?" I asked.

"Yes, I did. I have been through fertility treatments, and nothing seemed to work. I was supposed to go through one last procedure, but I never did. I just gave up."

"That may have been the procedure that was needed," I told her.

"It may have, but I just got discouraged. Your father didn't seem to care whether I could have his child or not. I was starting to think he didn't want me to be pregnant anyway. Which is why when I was unable to conceive, it didn't faze him." I could see the tears welling up in her eyes.

"I think he would have been happy if you had gotten pregnant with a boy."

"Why do you think that?"

"Because growing up, he always treated me like I was a boy and one day he told me he wished that I was his son instead of his daughter," I confessed.

"Well, that's his loss because you have grown to be a bright young lady. And you're a great daughter."

"Thank you, and I'm just getting brighter and brighter every day."

"You got that right. And here we are." We pulled up at a restaurant that was packed with cars. Getting out, we walked to the entrance and entered the place.

"Wow, this place is packed."

"Yes, this place is always packed, no matter what day of the week it is."

We were seated at our table and as we went to sit down, we realized that the restaurant was set up buffet style. We both laughed at the blonde moment we just had and walked over to the buffet and filled our plates with food. After being satisfied with our selection of foods, we walked back over to our table that was away from most of the people in the restaurant. I'd picked the table on purpose because I wanted to talk to her in private about the robbery. I knew that I could trust her with my life after everything that we had gone through together. Besides, I needed advice on what to do once I got back home.

"I have something to tell you, but before I tell you, please promise not to flip out on me and become hysterical about this situation," I said nervously.

"I can't promise you I won't be hysterical, but I will promise to give you the best advice for the situation," Alice said honestly. I nodded my head, accepting that.

"Well, a few weeks ago, my friend Lily did the unthinkable. She robbed a bank and now it seems that I'm an accomplice to it because she came to the bank with me. Only I went in first because I was there to deposit a check. Unbeknownst to me, Lily had other plans, surprising me and all of the other people at the bank by robbing it." Alice sat back with a look of disbelief.

"Go on," she encouraged.

"Long story short, Lily shot and killed the security officer that was trying to stop her from getting away with the money. I'm so scared that when all of this comes out, no one will believe that I didn't know what was going on and I will be in a lot of trouble. She shot all of the cameras out inside the bank, not taking into consideration the footage that the surrounding businesses may have picked up. It would show her getting out of my car and me getting in that same car when I left the scene. I'm no snitch so when the cops questioned me when it happened, I lied to them. My gut is telling me that Lily is trying to turn this whole thing around and say that it was me or my idea."

"You have to beat her at her own game. If your gut is telling you something then you need to listen because nine times out of ten, what you're feeling is right. Don't go to authorities because you don't know all of the facts, but you need to prepare yourself for what could come," Alice said.

"And how do I prepare myself?" I asked with teary eyes.

"You need to get Lily on recording discussing the events of what happened that day. You need every detail to be sure every angle is covered. Don't let her see it coming, play along with her. This is a very dangerous game that you are about to play. If you need me, I'm only a phone call away." Her reassurance was everything in this moment.

"What do you think the cops will do to me for lying to them?" I asked.

"You will probably be charged with obstruction of justice because you did know what had happened inside of the bank just like everyone else that was present. But that's the worst that would happen," Alice gave me her honest opinion. After our talk we got ready to leave the restaurant. I was flying back to Dallas the next morning.

"I can't get over how beautiful your home is." I complimented her house for the second time since I'd been there.

"I worked so hard for this after leaving your father. Sometimes I can't believe that all of this is mine. I pray and thank God every day for blessing me with a better life. This is your home too and you are welcome here anytime. Speaking of home, what are your plans for your relationship with Christian? Have you thought about going back?"

"Yes, actually, I know what I'm going to do. I feel like he's shown his true colors and I've given more chances than I should have before I left his home. With our relationship still being fresh, I can only imagine how it would be years from now. I'm not sticking around to find out how, so my mind is made up. I refuse to let another man mistreat me; my dad did enough damage. I'm going to have a talk with him when I get back and bring this relationship to a close." Alice nodded her head, agreeing with me.

"My home is your home and if you ever need somewhere to go, just know that I'm always here for you. If Texas bipolar weather isn't working for you, you can always come to Hot Lanta!" We shared a laugh and Alice kissed me on my forehead before telling me to go get some rest before I had to catch my flight in a few hours.

CHAPTER EIGHTEEN

Babygirl

The next day, my plane landed back in Dallas. Christian had been calling and texting me every hour. I finally texted him back and agreed to meet him later for drinks. That wasn't enough for him because he then begged me to come over to his house for a small gathering with a few of his friends. At first, I hesitated to text him back about the invitation, but I finally did and agreed. I knew I was going to bring Lily with me if she wasn't too busy.

Christian texted me a smile emoji and I put my phone away and headed to my vehicle. All I wanted to do was get back to Lily's house and get some much needed rest. The only way that would happen is if Lily didn't have company over. I opened the door to the small apartment and surprisingly, Lily wasn't home. Finally, some peace and quiet, I thought to myself. I went into the bathroom to start my shower before going to sleep. Just as I was walking back into the livingroom, Lily entered the apartment.

"Hey chick, how was your trip?" She asked.

"Girl it was good. My stepmother is on a road to success, and I couldn't be any happier. Now I'm tired and need some rest but later, do you want to ride with me to Christian's get together? I plan to break it off with him tonight too. I just can't do it anymore," I said.

"Yes of course, I will go with you tonight. I'm not doing anything; it will be fun. And try not to hurt Christian's feelings too badly."

In the livingroom, I grabbed my duffle bag to bring to the bathroom with me. I didn't want her snooping through my bag and seeing what all I had. Before boarding the plan, Alice had taken me to the store to get a small recorder to wear under my clothes. I would use it to record Lily confessing to the robbery and murder. I figured it was best to get myself dressed now so that I could conceal the camera without her looking over my shoulder. Once I was sure that it was well hidden, I walked past her room and laid down on the couch, falling asleep instantly.

We eventually woke up about the same time. Lily walked into the living room puzzled by me already being dressed.

"Why are you already dressed, you leaving without me?"

"Oh no, I decided to just go ahead and get dressed so that I could sleep longer. All I have left to do is brush my teeth again, brush my hair, beat my face, and we can be out," I told Lily.

"I still don't understand why you would get dressed and sleep in your clothes." She gave me a confused look.

"It's nothing Lily. I was just tired from my trip and wanted more rest that's all," I lied. "Come on, go get dressed." Hesitantly, she turned around and went back to her room. It didn't take her long to put herself together.

"I'm all ready now," Lily said as she came out prancing around. We both took shots of gin and she topped it off by playing in her nose, wanting her extra high.

Satisfied with our looks, we jumped in my Rover and headed to Christian's house. Once we arrived Lily was acting a little different but still said that Christian's house was fat and that he was living large now. I wondered what she meant about "living large now" as if she knew him before I had introduced the two. She pointed out the black Jag that sat in his driveway, letting me know that she knew someone who drove that car.

"Things are about to get real interesting," she said through gritted teeth.

We both stepped out of the truck, and I made sure the microphone was still hidden and my phone was fully charged. Christian greeted the both of us at the door, giving Lily a quick once over before focusing back on me. He gave me a tight hug and kissed my neck, whispering in my ear how much he missed me. I gave a small smile and allowed him to usher me into the house. The night was going so well, with Christian playing me close, dancing all on me.

He kept hinting at me staying the night with him but we both knew that wasn't about to happen. I kept dancing with him though and dodged any other advances. I was focused on Christian, but I also watched Lily from a distance, taking a count of her drinks, measuring when she was good and drunk in order to get the confession I needed. I walked with Christian outside to the balcony, this was my chance to break it off with him.

"Hey, you having a good time?" He asked me.

"Yeah, but we need to talk."

"Okay, come on." He led me by my hand, further out on the balcony.

"Christian, I'm no longer happy with our relationship. I feel that we should just cool off for a while," I came right out with it.

"Cool off? Naw I'm not feeling that mami, you cooled off long enough. How much more do I have to cool off for the mistakes that I've made?"

"Apologizing isn't enough, I want to see results before I jump back in," I told him. I could tell that he was starting to get agitated, so I backed away. Looking around, he picked up a lone, glass beer bottle from the table and threw it over the balcony, causing it to shatter.

I looked past him, into the house, and watched as people began to leave when they saw Christian coming out of character. I could see that they knew shit was about to go left. I turned and ran back into the house where I saw Lily and Christian's homeboy standing there.

"Come on, Lily, we have to go before he really starts losing his mind." I went to grab Lily's arm in the same fashion as she had done mine at the mall that time, but she didn't budge.

"Bitch, you're not going anywhere," Christian gritted, barging into the house.

"Lily lets...go," I spoke in a stern tone. I waited for her to move, reading the hesitance all in her body language. I didn't know what she had going on, but she was really pissing me off.

"I said..." I spun around and Christian's eyes met mine, halting his next works.

"Christian, I am leaving, and if you try to stop me, I will be forced to call the authorities. Let's not embarrass ourselves more than we already have okay. Come on." I cut my eyes at Lily and she finally walked towards the exit with me on her heels. Once we made it out to my truck, I didn't bother unlocking the doors before I was on her head. "What the hell is your problem? You see this man in a full rage and you're standing around amongst the rest of the spectators just watching the show, Lily. What the hell were you thinking?!" I was beside myself.

"My name is Lillian," she said with a faraway look in her eyes.

"What are you talking about?"

"You called me Lily. I'm correcting you and letting you know that my name is Lillian, Lillian Haynes."

"Okay, I'm confused and right now, I don't have time to figure out what name you want to go by. Let's just get in the car and get back to your place. My head is hurting, and I would hate for Christian to come out here and get more shit started."

"Babygirl, you would want to know exactly who I am. It may help you accept what's going to happen to you a little better when it happens."

"Lily, you're talking in riddles. Are you high?"

She snickered. "I took my bump back at the house and that's been it. I'm not sober but I'm in the right state of mind to say what's been on my heart."

"I don't have time for this shit," I let out, frustrated and mentally at my wits end. I didn't even care about what I'd set out to do, I just wanted to lay down.

"It's funny you speak about time, because that's exactly what you'll be doing once the police find out that you were the mastermind behind that bank robbery." The smirk on Lily's face made my heart stop and my face contorted.

"Lily, you know I had absolutely nothing to do with that! That was all your doing."

"Hmm, was it? You were the one who drove to pull the caper, were you not?"

"I..."

"Save it," she cut me off, "no need to plead your case to me, sweetie. Everything is already in the works, and they'll be here in a minute to get their number one suspect... you."

Tears fell from my eyes freely, as the betrayal cut me like a knife. Here she was actually admitting out loud to setting me up. Although I knew she was up to no good, for her to admit it without a care in the world broke me. "Why, Lily? I loved you like a sister. We were down together, and I held you down when you had no one!" My voice went up an octave and cracked.

"Ohh, poor, Babygirl. It's always about what's been done to you. WHAT ABOUT WHAT YOUR SNAKE ASS FATHER DID TO ME?!" Her tone matched mine and the fire in her eyes couldn't be missed.

I stood there hurt and now confused as to what my dad had to do with this. "I...I don't understand."

"Oh, God, please with this innocent act. You were spawn from a no good pimp, you know the game, Cameron."

"What game? How do you know my father?"

"I not only know your father but that no good bitch you call a step-mother, your precious Alice, I know her too. You see, I'm not the young girl I approached you as years ago. I'm actually 36 years old, a grown ass woman. Long story short, your father owes me. Both he and Alice pimped me out for years and never saw to it that I got what I was owed. For a while after I'd left him, I thought about how I could get my money and then he vanished. The first time I'd seen him in a long time was the night that he snatched Alice's stupid ass up and left you behind. How did I know you were his daughter? I mean you've looked at yourself in the mirror. You look just like the bastard."

"So, you got close to me for what? You thought you were gonna get some money? I was in the same fucked up position as you when you met me."

"You're right about that. It stopped being about the money and more about the game. That's what all this shit has been to me. I wanted to get close to you, and what better way than to disguise myself as a runaway teen with no family that loved her. Getting close to you and put you in some unsavory places with some unsavory people. I could've gotten my revenge by doing you physical harm a long time ago, but seeing you go to jail for a crime you didn't commit just feels so much like victory." She smiled wildly and I went to lunge at her when I heard two shots go off. POP POP!

I went to take cover behind my truck and watched as the remaining guests scrambled out of Christian's house, almost toppling over each other. My next move was to hop in my truck and peel out, but I didn't dare move in fear of letting Lily out of my sight. I could see her crouched down on the passenger side of my truck. People hopped in their cars and before they could exit Christian's driveway, three patrol cars were making their way in.

Everything moved so fast, I felt like I was on set of a movie, only this was my real life. It was crazy how fast they'd come but with Christian living in an upscale neighborhood, I didn't expect there to be much of a wait either. The officers jumped out of their cars, guns drawn, not bothering to assess the situation.

"Everyone, put your hands where we can see them, NOW!" One of the officers in the first vehicle yelled out. All hands were raised immediately.

"Officer," I heard Lily call out, "this woman has a gun in her car and I'm afraid for my life."

I couldn't see her face, but I was sure that if looks could kill, she'd be one dead bitch right now. I couldn't put into words how I was feeling, and I was so shocked, I couldn't verbally defend myself. One of the officers walked slowly towards me after requesting I move back from my truck. Still in a trance, I did as he said.

"Ma'am, do you have any weapons in this vehicle?" He asked, while resting his hand on my door.

"No, sir, I don't." My voice was steady, but the nervousness was apparent. I was sure he took that as a sign of guilt.

"Yes, she does," Lily let out. "It's under the floor mat, on the driver's side."

The officer stared at me, and I stared back. I took another step back and nodded with my head, giving non-verbal permission for him to search. He opened the door, and I checked the spot where Lily said the gun was. I could've died when he pulled out a black firearm and held it up for me to see.

"That's not mine, I swear to God!"

"It is, and she threatened to kill me just before you all arrived." Lily was laying it on so thick, I was tempted to grab the gun from the officer and shoot her stupid ass.

"Sir, please, that gun is not mine and I can prove that she's setting me up."

"We can talk about it down at the station. Ma'am, you're under arrest. Clarke," he called out to another officer, "would you come and Mirandize this woman."

"Miss," he said to Lily, "I need you to walk around the truck slowly and over to me with your hands up." I watched Lily's steps as she walked around the car until she was just a few feet away from me.

This bitch was playing the role so well, she almost had me convinced. Looking past her, I watched as Christian was escorted from his house in cuffs and thought to myself, what the hell had he done? Was he the one shooting? I listened as the female officer read me my rights and as soon as I felt those bracelets click on my wrist, my while body went numb. "It's not my gun! I swear, she's setting me up, I can prove it!" Hearing my statement, Lily now rocked the confused look. "I have everything on recording."

TO BE CONTINUED...

A Setup For Revenge 2
Coming Soon

CHAPTER ONE

"John Thompson, please report to the principal's office."

The class went silent and I looked up to find everyone staring at me. My teacher, a robust black woman in her mid-thirties said okay, made her way to her desk and began writing my pass.

Damn! What they calling me to the office for? I know I ain't did shit wrong. I put my stuff in my book bag and walked to the teacher's desk to get a hall pass, and couldn't help but notice two of my female classmates pointing at me whispering.

She finished writing the pass and handed it to me. "If you don't come back, have a nice day."

"Okay, Ms. Bell."

Exiting the classroom, I made my way up the hall to the front office, racking my brain in thought of anything I could've done wrong, but drew a blank. I knew I had done nothing wrong, but being young and black in Chicago, you weren't innocent until proven guilty. You were guilty until proven innocent. Ms. Bell was my favorite teacher. She had done so much to keep me out of trouble this year. I didn't want to let her down, and even worse, I didn't want to fail mama. We were all we had and she was counting on me.

I don't know what it was, but before I got to the office I knew it was nothing good. I walked in and handed the pass to the secretary, an older black woman with glasses, looking like someone's strict auntie. She looked at it above the rim of her glasses, shifted her eyes back to me and told me to go straight into Mr. Thomas' office. He was the school principal, ironically the only white one in our school district. I headed to the back and walked into his office to find him strokin' his thick mustache behind his mahogany desk. In front of him in one of the two chairs on the opposite side was a white woman that I didn't know.

"Oh, here's John now. How are you doing today?" Mr. Thomas gestured towards the empty seat.

I made my way over and sat next to the white lady, taking note of the gleam on Mr. Thomas's bald head from the bright lights above us. "I'm not in trouble, am I, Mr. Thomas?"

"No, no. Umm. This is Ms. Long. I was just telling her about how I've only heard good things about you even before you started school here."

At the mention of her name, Ms. Long smoothed out her burgundy slacks and wisped a strand of her long brown hair behind her ear to reveal her pearl earrings. She had to be at least thirty, but what did she want with me?

I looked at Mr. Thomas for a few seconds, waiting to see if he was going to tell me what this was about and he continued. "I'm going to leave the two of you to talk. If you need anything, I'll be right outside the door."

Mr. Thomas got up, left the room, and as soon as the door closed the lady began. "As you know, I'm Ms. Long. I work for the Illinois Department of Children and Family Service."

"Me and my Mama don't need no family service, so…"

"John, maybe before today that would've been true, but an hour ago my office got a call from the Chicago Police Department and was informed that there was a homicide."

"Man, what do any of that got to do with me!" This lady was starting to piss me off. "Can you get to the point so I can go back to class?"

"John, your mother was killed today in an attempted robbery…" and that was the last thing I heard.

———

What's happening? What's going on? I could hear voices, but all I saw was black. I slowly began to blink my eyes open and found that Ms.

Long and I were no longer the only people in the office. She, the school nurse, and Mr. Thomas surrounded me. I looked back at Ms. Long, and when she looked back down at me it hit me. I was filled with rage. "You lyin' bitch!"

I jumped up and tried to swing on Ms. Long, but somebody grabbed me by my shoulders and stopped me short. I tried to shake them off but whoever it was just tightened their grip.

"Let me the fuck go!"

"I won't do that until you calm down." It was Mr. Thomas.

"I'm not tryin' to hear that. This lady lying, saying my mama got killed!"

"I'm sorry John, but she is not lying."

"Get off of me!" I continued to struggle, but it was useless.

"John!"

"Fuck that!" Try as I might, I was powerless to escape his grasp. Just as powerless as I am to bring mama back.

That did it. I lost all the fight in me. I realized now my mama was really gone and I'll never see her again. I crumbled to the ground and started crying. They handed me tissues and let me have my time. Moments later I dried my eyes.

"I'm very sorry for your loss. I know it's painful." Ms. Long handed me more tissues. "You might not understand this now, but always remember, tough times don't last but tough people do."

She squatted down and hugged me, holding me the way a mother would, making me cry harder. I had to get it together. It was time to grow up. I stopped crying, wiped my eyes, and decided from this point on no one would see me shed another tear.

———

We pulled up in front of the tan brick apartment building I've been living in for the last eight months, outside of which a small group of drug dealers were posted, making hand over fist plays. The sky was a cold grey, adding to the paleness of the hood. There was no grass, only dirty littered up concrete as far as the eyes could see. As I got out of the car and started walking up the walkway with Ms. Long, I got a sick feeling in my stomach thinking about going inside and it being empty of my mama's presence. It was a shame. This was the last year in the '90s. She almost made it to the new millennium. Born in the '60s, I know she would've liked that.

I must have slowed down because Ms. Long stopped. "Honey, if you want, you can stay in the car and I can get you enough stuff for a few weeks. We'll come back sometime after the funeral to get the rest."

"No, I can do it, now. I'm okay."

The first door didn't need a key so we walked straight in and started up the stairs. We got to the second-floor landing, and there were people about drinking, smoking, shooting dice and talking casually as though today were a regular day and my mama didn't just get killed. Some of them were my mama's so-called friends, yet they acted like they didn't care. They saw me, put their heads down, and turned away. I didn't feel no type of way. I ain't expect nothing less of them.

I took my key out, opened our apartment door and smelled the sweet scent of my mama's perfume. My eyes filled with tears, but I wasn't about to let them fall.

"Do you have any suitcases or bags to pack your stuff in?"

"Yeah, we got some."

"Okay, do you want me to help you with the packing?"

"Naw, I can do it. I'll let you know if I need any help."

"Well, I guess I'll wait out here."

I went to my room so I could get all my stuff together. The first thing I saw was an envelope on my bed with Papa written across it. Papa was the nickname that my mama always used, mainly when nobody else was around. I sat on the bed, picked up the envelope, and held it to my nose. Closing my eyes, I inhaled her scent once more, before exhaling and opening the letter to read.

Papa,

I love you more than life itself. I know the last year or so I haven't been at my best and I'm truly sorry for that, but above all things, I'm sorry you saw me doing drugs. It has taken a while to realize that this ain't the life I want to live. I want what's best for us. I am done with the drugs. I'm going to try and get my old job back. I cashed my check and I'm taking twenty dollars out for a bus pass. I'm leaving you the two hundred dollars that's left. I'll be late coming home so fix yourself something to eat or wait and take me out to eat. No matter what happens, remember, I will forever love you! Kisses and Hugs.

Mama

"I love you too, mama."

I sat and reread the letter a few more times before I could put it down. My mama wrote I love you and I'm sorry all over the card and stuck the money inside.

I grabbed my book bag and went to the closet where we kept the shoebox my mama had been saving since she was 18 years old. No matter what, every time she got some money, she put some up. In our old neighborhood, I would cut grass and wash cars to make money and put up. I opened the door and caught sight of myself in the mirror that hung on the back, just inside. I paused and stared at myself. Something was different. I looked like I had aged ten years since I left for school that morning. It wasn't a hair thing, either. A short cut had always been my style. I was still that dark skin kid with a big nose, but my medium build seemed deflated. It made me feel defeated, or maybe me feeling defeated was causing me to look this way. I had to check that shit. Hunching my shoulders back, I held my chin high, took a deep breath and continued to where the shoebox was stashed. When I took the lid off the shoebox, I couldn't believe my eyes. The money I thought would be there was nowhere close to the amount we had saved. I found the slip that said how much should've been in there, close to fifteen G's. But when I counted it, there was only four hundred thirty, leaving me six hundred thirty to start over with. I hurried and put it in my bag. I then found the other bags and packed my stuff. Ms. Long told me to leave my mama's stuff, but I packed up all the books and pictures she had.

"Okay, are you sure you have everything you want?" Ms. Long asked as she put some papers she was writing on back in her briefcase and stood up.

"Pretty much, except maybe the T.V and radio. Can I take them with me?"

"I don't know about that. We'll have to see if the family that takes you in will allow that. They might already have them at their house. If they don't mind, I'll double back and bring them to you."

"Hold up, what do you mean by the family that takes me in? I thought you was taking me home with you. Why can't I just stay here?"

"I thought you understood what was happening. Let me clear it up, you're going to a foster home; people who are willing to take minors in that have nowhere else to go. You could stay there for months, years or they might even adopt you and become your new family. I'm a caseworker, I make sure that you're placed in a stable home. You can't live with me, and there are too many reasons why you cannot stay here by yourself, but mainly because you wouldn't have a legal guardian."

"Alright. Can we just go now?"

We carried all the bags to the front door from the bedroom. "Stay here while I take what I can out to the car," she said.

She walked off with the first couple bags and no sooner than she bent the corner did the door to the apartment across the hall open and a man stepped out. "Man, what's up lil homie, you good?"

It was Corn, the tall, light brown skin guy with the short curly 'fro. He had been my neighbor for as long as I could remember, and as always, he maintained his razor lining. He was slim, and though his mustache was thin, his pockets were far from it. Ms. Kelly was his mother, and though she owned the building he was living in, he controlled all the drugs being sold on the block.

"Yeah, I'm cool, Corn."

"Man, I'm sorry to hear about what happened to your ol' G, real talk." He waited but continued when he saw I ain't have nothing to say. "I don't know what they about to do with you but if you ever need anything, my mom lives here, and..." he went in his pocket to get a pen and piece of paper and wrote something, then handed it to me.

"Here's my phone number. Don't lose it. Call whenever. Okay, lil homie?"

"Yeah but..." I didn't get to finish because Ms. Long was back.

"Let me help y'all with some of these heavy bags so Miss Lady ain't got to keep hitting all the stairs."

"I would appreciate that. Thank you."

"They call me Corn, and it ain't no problem."

He picked up all but three bags and gave Ms. Long a smirk.

She turned away and grabbed two of the bags. "John, lock up and bring the last bag down when you're done."

CHAPTER TWO

Ms. Long told me I was going to a suburb called Addison which was like thirty or something minutes away from Chicago. I sat back and thought about how messed up my day has been. I had a lot of questions I knew wouldn't be answered. I wish I knew why someone would want to kill my mama. She never did nothing to nobody. Where is the God she said was always watching over us?

I felt the car slowing down and opened my eyes as we were going down an off-ramp. I looked out the window and thought about how nice it looked. I was used to the city and this was far from that.

"This the place I'm going to be livin'?"

"Yes, this is the town and the house shouldn't be far from here."

"What's up with me goin' to school?"

"I'm not sure right now, but we should have you back in school in about a week or so. From what I hear they have a real nice high school."

"What about other kids?"

"What do you mean?"

"I'm saying though, is there other kids going to be staying in the house I'm going to?"

"Oh, yes, I think my reports say they have two other children. Here we are, now, so you can meet them for yourself."

I have been looking at how big the houses were since we turned on the street, but I didn't think I would be living in any of them. I was definitcly in the suburbs. The lawns were green and manicured, there were white people out and about walking dogs, and there were Audi A2's, Honda HR-V's, and BMW X5's sitting in the driveways. We parked in front of this big ass brick house that looked like something straight out a movie. "This the house I'm staying at?"

"Yes, this is it. Are you ready?"

I really didn't see it as if I had a choice. "Yeah, I guess so."

Before we could get out the car the front door opened and a short lady came out smiling. She looked like a nice person and her smile almost made me want to smile. Almost. She was five-foot-three, and wasn't fat, but wasn't skinny either. A little lighter than me, she was a peanut butter complexion with long shiny hair. Next, a tall dude came out and for a second, I thought he was Scottie Pippen that played for the Bulls, number 33, I think. But the closer he got, I could tell he wasn't.

Still smiling the lady approached us. "How are you doing, young man? I am Mom and..."

I didn't even let her finish. "Whatcha mean? You ain't my Mama, and I'm not calling you that!"

She stopped smiling and looked at me like I was crazy; that's when Ms. Long started talking.

"Umm, they must have forgot to fill you in on the details of John's situation." The lady shook her head. "Today John's mother was murdered so maybe something else besides mom would be better for a while."

"Oh, I'm sorry to hear that. I'm not trying to take your mom's place, you can call me Mrs. Davis." She looked in the tall dude's direction. "And this is my husband, Mister Davis. Our other children are still at their after-school programs, but they should be home soon. In the meantime, why don't we get your things inside and get you settled in?"

After every bag was out the car and in my new room, Ms. Long left. Mrs. Davis went on to cook dinner, leaving me and Mr. Davis to unpack and have a "little chat" as he put it.

"Now, John, you are excused for that incident earlier, but I swear if you ever raise your god damn voice at me or my wife again, I will beat you so bad, you will wish that you was the one that died, today, instead of your mother. Understood?"

"Yeah, I guess, Mr. Davis."

"It ain't no guessing to it. Try me if you want. Another thing, you will call my wife mom and me dad because that is who we are in this house. Any child that we allow to live here when we don't have to will refer to us as such."

"I didn't ask to come live here."

"But your little bitch ass is here and since you got such a smart mouth, why don't you stand up and see if you a man?"

This dude was big as hell, so what I look like standing up to fight him? I stayed seated. "Man, I'm not no bitch."

"I see you ain't no man either because you still sitting down. I'll tell you this once, it is only enough room for one man in this house and that's me. So, whenever you feel that you're a man, one of us got to go and it won't be me. Now, get this room together before dinner."

I wanted to cry as soon as he closed the door. I didn't though. I held it in because it wasn't going to make it better. Maybe Ms. Long could find me another place to live; anywhere away from this hell house. This chat made me realize that hell is where Ms. Long has just left me- Mr. and Mrs. Davis were the Devil.

For now, I gotta go with the flow, but one way or the other I'm leaving this place.

Available Now
on all online retail book platforms!!

OTHER BOOKS BY

URBAN AINT DEAD

Tales 4rm Da Dale

By **Elijah R. Freeman**

The Hottest Summer Ever

By **Elijah R. Freeman**

Despite The Odds

By **Juhnell Morgan**

The Swipe

By **Toōla**

Hittaz 1 & 2

By **Lou Garden Price, Sr**

Good Girls Gone Rogue

By **Manny Black**

The State's Witness

By **Kyiris Ashley**

Ridin' For You

By **Telia Teanna**

COMING SOON FROM

URBAN AINT DEAD

The Hottest Summer Ever 2
By **Elijah R. Freeman**

THE G-CODE
By **Elijah R. Freeman**

How To Publish A Book From Prison
By **Elijah R. Freeman**

Tales 4rm Da Dale 2
By **Elijah R. Freeman**

Ridin' For You, Too
By **Telia Teanna**

Hittaz 3
By **Lou Garden Price, Sr.**

The State's Witness 2
By **Kyiris Ashley**

The Swipe 2
By **Toōla**

A Setup For Revenge 2
By **Ashley Williams**

Good Girl Gone Rogue 2

By **Manny Black**

Charge It To The Game

By **Nai**

Despite The Odds 2

By **Juhnell Morgan**

BOOKS BY

URBAN AINT DEAD's C.E.O
Elijah R. Freeman

Triggadale 1, 2 & 3

Tales 4rm Da Dale

The Hottest Summer Ever

Murda Was The Case 1 & 2

Follow

Elijah R. Freeman

On Social Media

FB: Elijah R. Freeman

IG: @the_future_of_urban_fiction